DAUGHTER OF THE STORM

ALSO BY ALDEN GLOBE

Fiction

Daughter of the Cloud*: A Maps Private Value Thriller*
Audiobook available everywhere audiobooks are sold
Hija de la Nube, Spanish translation

Daughter of the Storm*: A Maps Private Value Thriller*

Daughter of Mars: *A Maps Private Value Thriller* (Coming 2025)

Nonfiction

Carry On*: Notes on Business Travel*

SMART*: Notes for Product Managers*

Enterprise Content Services: *Managing Corporate Knowledge*

Managing Knowledge*: A Practical Web-based Approach*

DAUGHTER OF THE STORM

A MAPS PRIVATE VALUE THRILLER

ALDEN GLOBE

"There are good ships, and there are wood ships, the ships that sail the sea. But the best ships are friendships. May they always be."
—Scottish toast, traditional

Published January 2024.

Contact the author: Alden.globe@gmail.com

"I must only warn you of one thing. You have become a different person in the course of these years. For this is what the art of archery means: a profound and far-reaching contest of the archer with himself."
—*Zen in the Art of Archery*, Eugen Herrigel

"Life is a good teacher and a good friend. Things are always in transition, if we could only realize it."
—*When Things Fall Apart: Heart Advice for Difficult Times*, Pema Chödrön

6th UNIPCC GLOBAL CLIMATE ASSESSMENT
2023

"**A.1** Human activities, principally through emissions of greenhouse gases, have unequivocally caused global warming, with global surface temperature reaching 1.1°C above 1850–1900 in 2011–2020. Global greenhouse gas emissions have continued to increase, with unequal historical and ongoing contributions arising from unsustainable energy use, land use and land-use change, lifestyles and patterns of consumption and production across regions, between and within countries, and among individuals (high confidence)."

"**A.2** Widespread and rapid changes in the atmosphere, ocean, cryosphere and biosphere have occurred. Human-caused climate change is already affecting many weather and climate extremes in every region across the globe. This has led to widespread adverse impacts and related losses and damages to nature and people (high confidence)."

"**C.1** Climate change is a threat to human well-being and planetary health (very high confidence). There is a rapidly closing window of opportunity to secure a liveable and sustainable future for all (very high confidence). The choices and actions implemented in this decade will have impacts now and for thousands of years (high confidence)."

CHARACTERS BY INSTITUTION

MAPS PRIVATE VALUE. MALLORCA
Rave Maps, Owner & Principal Value Engineer
Maitland "Mait" Orleans, U. S. Navy, Ret.

NC3 NATIONAL CYBERCRIME COORDINATION. CANADA
Kate Tong, Chief

THE LODGE AT CHAA CREEK. BELIZE
Candelaria "Cande" Teresita, Guide

US FOREST SERVICE. USFS ROCKY MOUNTAIN R2
Chance "CC" Cole, Type 1 Interagency Hotshot Handcrew Leader

LADY ELLIOT ISLAND ECO RESORT. AUSTRALIA
Archie Harper, Biologist.

GLOBAL MIXED INDUSTRY SERVICE ASSOCIATION. GRENADA
Bellony LaMarque, CEO
Max Tiburon, Lobbyist in Brussels. USMC, Ret.

BIOSAFETY RESEARCH LABORATORY. SKOPJE, MACEDONIA
Stojan "Traj" Trajkovski, Sr. Gene Editing Research Associate

CONTENTS

CLIFFHANGER 9
PORT DE SÓLLER 11
KINETIC SOLUTION 22
FORECAST CALLS FOR PAIN 25
REGENERATIVE VALUE TERRAIN 35
INFINITE MONKEY THEOREM 37
HEAD IN THE CLOUDS 43
DOESN'T' MAKE DOLLARS, DOESN'T MAKE SENSE 59
AIR 62
FIRE 73
WATER 86
END OF THE RAINBOW 96
RAY OF SUNSHINE 102
EYE OF THE STORM 105
BARCELONA 109
LOW-RISE GENES 114
SMITE FLAT THE THICK ROTUNDITY O' THE WORLD! 119
STORMCLOUD 129
SOLO 132
DAUGHTER OF THE STORM 136
SATORI 151
SOURCES 153
ACKNOWLEDGMENTS 157
COMING 2025: DAUGHTER OF MARS 160
ABOUT THE AUTHOR 164

CLIFFHANGER

Cycling focuses the mind. Next pedal stroke. Next breath. Keep cadence. Watch the road. Ease pressure on wrists and neck. Heels out. Elbows in. Change gears. Check speed. Repeat.

Mait Orleans continued pedaling. She was making her way up a steep, narrow stretch of twisty MA-10, Mallorca's most scenic and difficult ride. Mait focused on her breathing, tackling her third large hill. MA-10 was as challenging a ride as the guidebook suggested. She had been passed by pelotons—uniformed groups of riders working in synchronized cadence— from several countries. She had passed a few lone cyclists like herself as well, each intent on reaching the top of the next rise.

Mait reached a plateau running along the top of a cliff. Feeling a small thrill of victory, she paused to step off the bike and stretch, enjoying a spectacular view of the ocean. She saw choppy seas driven by a breeze from the northwest, and the air smelled clean and sweet. The silence was pierced by screeches from a pair of the islands thirty-nine rare Bonelli's eagles that floated lazily overhead, riding powerful updrafts racing up the cliff.

Mait got back on the bike, setting off once more. She had become used to how close cars came to riders on this route. Sometimes a sideview mirror would be inches from her handlebars; there was no maneuvering room on the narrow road. Fortunately, drivers in Mallorca are accustomed to avoiding cyclists and take great care passing.

It didn't strike Mait as unusual then when one more vehicle, a Spanish-made SEAT Ateca SUV, pulled alongside. No other cars or cyclists were in sight. It took just a tap from the side view mirror to flick Mait's handlebars right, sending her off the road to the cliff's edge. No guardrails here. It happened so fast, Mait was unable to react. She fought to correct her steering, risking a glance in the car window. No one inside. Driverless car.

Her next surprise came as her front tire crunched over the lip, pulling her, bike and all, over the edge. She was falling.

Mait Orleans, a highly analytical former naval officer, not a person to be trifled with, found herself feeling detached from the situation. Instead of screaming, she began reflecting on the failure cascade that led to her being here. As she tumbled through space, she felt time slow. She began thinking. Could she sort out what she might do to mitigate this fatal situation? Could she find something, anything, that might help turn it to her advantage?

PORT DE SÓLLER

Rave Maps, the world's greatest value engineer, had been staring at her computer for hours. She was trying to figure out how to visualize the value a customer might realize by turning core IT operations over to a specialized outsourcing firm.

The client, an oil-field services company, needed an efficient method for handling seismic survey data because they were seeking the fastest way to identify patterns in the Earth's crust leading to rich sources of helium.

Helium deposits were the result of radioactive decay and were often located in old natural gas mines. Helium molecules shed heat quickly, making it ideal for manufacturing semiconductor chips. A thin layer of helium drained heat from the silicon wafers while integrated circuits were etched on their surface. These chips were critical for computers as well as cell phones, automobiles, medical devices, and credit cards, and demand had exploded.

Rave assembled graphs illustrating the monthly cost of a cloud subscription compared with the high cost of building a new data center stuffed with thousands of computer servers. Not to mention the environmental impact of yet one more large, energy-hungry industrial facility.

When Rave finished, she knew she'd built a compelling story financially, but it lacked in the emotional, life-changing hooks she liked to imbue in her value deliverables. They were *stories* after all, and what good was a story if the client wasn't emotionally attached to it? She needed to find a hook to drive her point home.

Mulling it over, knowing she needed something for a nontechnical audience of executive decision-makers, she felt an animation might make sense. Perhaps a two-minute video summarizing the challenge would do the trick.

Several hours into that effort, she realized she hadn't heard from Mait in some time. Not since Orleans had confirmed she was biking across northern Mallorca, part of an effort to survey a piece of property one of Rave's clients had expressed an interest in. Rave texted Mait. No response.

She decided to stretch and head outside for some air. "Ready for a walk, guys?" Ski Boot and Truffles, her loyal Shih Tzu mixes had been napping by her feet. At the word "walk," the dogs went to battle stations, ready to head out.

The three of them stepped out of the finca, a 170-year-old remodeled wood and stone farmhouse perched on a hill overlooking Port de Sóller. Mait had purchased the farmhouse three years ago. Large French doors opened to a secluded pool terrace. The backyard garden was lush with varieties of hardy plants thriving on the island, despite regular battering by strong sea breezes and being rooted in soil riddled with ocean salt. Sea fennels, saladines, and sea daisies bloomed here among clumped communities of thorny pads. Jardi Botanic de Sóller, a local botanical garden, categorized a thousand varieties of Balearic flora and fruit trees that thrived in the salty soil.

Several years ago, Mait explained to Rave what she wanted when she retired from the U.S. Department of State Diplomatic Security Service. "I need to shake things up, Rave. I'm thinking of a small farmhouse with a view of the ocean. I want to seek harmony, grow oranges, tend to bees, and raise fairy goats."

Mait invited Rave to join her on this quest for serenity over a luxurious afternoon tea at the Baccarat Hotel tearoom in New York after their last harrowing experience. Orleans had helped Maps defeat a crazed tech entrepreneur who managed to create a powerful AI that had been busy uploading the minds of the world's greatest subject matter experts. The AI focused on creating a cloud-based library of human wisdom, unfortunately killing its subjects during a process known as REPing, or Resurrection with Extreme Prejudice. The subjects died once the upload of their consciousness was complete.

Maps had been the only human who did manage to survive the REPing process, though enough of her mind had been captured and uploaded that a remarkable electronic twin had been created in the cloud, providing both beings an extraordinary experience for a brief time. Maps had been connected to a digital being she nicknamed Digital Maps, an AI with incredible intelligence and wide-ranging information capabilities.

Shortly after, that connection was severed by the AI itself when it determined it must destroy other AI projects before they ran amuck within different weapon systems. Once Digital Maps had acted to ensure it was the only advanced AI remaining on Earth, it had retired to contemplate many different potential futures for humanity from a secure, remote location on Mars.

As part of her healing journey, Rave set up shop in Mait's dream home in Mallorca back in 2024. One hundred and sixty miles southwest of Barcelona, Mallorca is one of the Balearic Islands, standing between Ibiza and Minorca, and home to the city of Palma. Port de Sóller, a one-hour train ride north of Palma, would be a new place for Rave to call home. Here she could unwind, recover, and plot out the next chapter in her life.

Rave often reminded herself to be fully present no matter where she was working. Through daily meditation with her Healthy Minds app, she'd become pretty good at raising her insight and awareness, integrating a lifetime of experience that had been spent in grueling ranch labor, years of military service, managing entrepreneurial start-ups, and now running a consulting business driven by the relentless pace of technology and changing customer demands that was worth $60 million.

Rave began thinking back over one of her recent long talks with Mait on the garden patio. Mait had asked her: "What is the most important advice you normally offer your clients?"

Rave had a ready answer: "Stay close to revenue and customers." Then she began explaining further. "In a world of data, software, and systems, how can anyone determine what the value of an IT investment is? You can't taste, touch, smell, or see most of these software solutions. They live buried deep in the 'IT stack' that makes things work at companies in systems ranging from mainframes to the cloud."

Mait interrupted her. "You're referring, I think, to what I've heard you call the 'Invisible World?' The backend logistics and technology supporting our consumer desires when we purchase online, post comments, or seek answers on our devices?"

"Exactly." Rave continued her monologue; now she was fired up. "Value is always in the eye of the beholder. *Always*. We dig through conversations, do research, conduct interviews, and try and get at what each customer wants. *Really* wants. It was usually something they could not give voice to; it's buried so deep. We probe and try coming at it in different ways. Value engineering is a mix of psychology, guesswork, and power of persuasion aimed at determining what each client considers valuable.

"We can ask questions like 'What do you need to make yourself more productive?' Executives and frontline staff are never able to answer that question. To answer would require continuous self-reflection and focus, and that's an effort few have the bandwidth to handle while performing daily work tasks. It falls to value engineers to figure out what that thing is and show it to them. Make it real. Help build excitement by letting clients know that future dream is achievable."

Mait picked up this thread: "That improvement could be a simple idea? Maybe saving time or reducing cost?"

"Yes," Rave went on. "Or it could be something harder to tease out, such as identifying what drives customer loyalty to a brand."

Rave looked over to the driveway. "For example, why do you drive an Audi RS e-tron GT? Does something about it make it more desirable to you than a BMW, Toyota, or Maserati? Or a Ford? Is there something about it that speaks to who you are inside? From the vehicle you drive, I can tell you're excited by passion, inspiration, and technology. You'll push boundaries. You're committed to sustainability, you prefer engineering tuned for performance. You're a demanding driver. Your choice underlines all these qualities."

Mait remained mute, thinking it over. Rave wasn't wrong.

Rave continued: "Individual consumer choices provide clues to what clients value and how they see themselves. In an organizational context, the desired thing may be improving quality or improving team morale. It could be creating a legacy for the leader, something to leave behind. It might include special entertainment, or a method for easing the performance of some task. It could be seeking inspiration that drives change. VEs—value engineers—strive to figure out what the 'thing' is. If we're successful, that effort can sometimes help elevate my company, Maps Private Value, to being the 'trusted advisor' to that leader or organization. Then our relationships and our firm prospers."

During yet another long talk on the terrace, Mait sought to explore Rave's thoughts on climate change, a topic that was perennially top of mind for her.

"Rave. You've said it's hard to determine the value of software solutions because you can't see, taste, or touch them. Isn't the need for climate action similar? Some people have a sense that things are changing. But it's hard for them to put a finger on what the problem is."

Rave paused to gather her thoughts, sipping coffee, looking out over the Mediterranean waves sparkling in the morning sun. Everywhere she traveled over the past decade, Rave had become aware of empirical evidence illustrating how serious changing trends were now, ranging from flood to drought, wildland fires to hurricanes and accelerating species loss. She began riffing off this thought.

"Farmers, wine growers, fishermen, and outdoor enthusiasts are aware of changes they see every day. They are seeking solutions and adapting to them in everything they do. There's no question what the problem is. It's driven by humans. Our growing fossil fuel emissions have been warming the Earth for over a century, and this has already impacted everything. Many don't see the impacts and don't think of these trends as connected. Mait, if you asked any of our friends here what they think the problem with climate is, what do you think they'd say?"

The two of them debated that question for hours. "Carbon emissions continue to rise; they haven't declined at all," Rave explained. "People across the world are raising living standards, which means more greenhouse gases, more power plants, more waste, and more pollution. The most urgently needed action to stop global temperature rise is to get off fossil fuel and develop other sources of energy."

Mait suggested it also made sense to begin thinking about alternatives in other areas. "The global population has grown by billions of people, impacting transportation, food production, conservation, consumption, and recycling. Failure to take the threats seriously will lead to more flooded coastal areas. Extreme weather. Failed crops and lost harvests. The list is growing pretty long."

Over the past five years, Rave had adopted everything she could think of to ensure she was walking her talk on climate. She was much more aggressive, holding herself and her firm to a higher Environmental, Social, and Governance (ESG) model. She encouraged her clients to do the same. While she continued working across the world, she now used journey optimization software to minimize her carbon footprint while traveling and bought carbon offsets to match the impact of her business flights. She defaulted to electric transportation options, sought carbon-neutral alternatives, worked remotely when she could, adopted sustainable best practices, and sought low-impact alternatives.

After moving to Mallorca, Rave began shopping less, recycling more, and thinking long-term about the impact of items she did purchase. She looked down, examining her short-sleeved, tan, straight-cut cotton blouse. She'd acquired the piece online from Sandro Secondhand in Paris, and it had become her summer go-to for its versatility, architectural lines, and freedom of movement. She looked up, examining the farmhouse itself. The comfortable, whitewashed structure was light and airy, blending color and textures producing an elegant, welcoming vibe. Leadership in Energy and Environment Design, or LEED, strategies shaped Maits' renovation. Locally sourced and eco-friendly materials, responsibly harvested woods, vintage furnishings, thoughtful use of daylight, improved water efficiency, and overall low energy consumption were all improvements Mait had invested in.

What was once a quaint little farmhouse was now truly a haven. Rave stood up and walked through the garden to a spot overlooking the port. A salty sea breeze, the choking *huoh huoh* call of seagulls engaged in a territorial dispute, and the heat of the sun cleared her mind. Distant sailboats cruised the coast. White sails, blue sky. It was another perfect moment, one of many she'd experienced since moving here.

Rave and Mait enjoyed additional breathtaking views from the terrace of nearby restaurant Mirador de ses Barques where they watched the sunset while gorging on fresh grilled dorado, rich arroz de pescado soup, and delicious catch-of-the-day prepared with rock salt infused with house-blend olive oil. Whatever was on the daily menu was worth celebrating, especially when they could top it all off with thick, creamy Mallorcan lemon tarts, another island specialty.

The pair of American expats had learned to pay close attention to many proud Mallorcan traditions, all of which served to celebrate the perpetually sunny Mediterranean character of their neighbors. These included religious festivals, celebrations, dances, music, fiestas, carnivals, handicrafts, local livestock exhibitions, confections, fairs, markets, and processions. There were also massive celebrations for the annual harvests of mushrooms, olives, honey, and pumpkins.

This pleasant anthropological pastime, exploring local customs and culture, happened to pair perfectly with research into autochthonous island wines. Bright sparkling wine, soft white wine, and juicy red wine flowed from a hundred small-batch vintners. Each managed to capture the island spirit, teasing it out of local vines thriving here in the sunny, dry climate, and expressed from grapes with evocative names: Callet, Gargollasa, Giró Ros, Vinater, and Jaumillo.

Wine wasn't the only beverage capturing island personality in a bottle. Rave and Mait had begun working to develop a taste for dark, bitter Palo Mallorca, or Palo, as the locals called it. The ancient herbal medicinal had evolved into an aperitif served on the rocks. Perhaps it was a cure for malaria as was originally thought. Or maybe it helped with digestion. Further detailed study would be required to reach a conclusion and position the strong liquor appropriately within their hierarchy of wellness and nutrition.

Rave ceased her reverie and returned inside, calling the dogs in and returning to her desk. Still nothing from Mait. This was beginning to concern her. She called once more. No answer.

It was too soon to really start worrying though. As a former naval officer, world traveler, martial artist, and security expert, Mait Orleans knew how to take care of herself.

Rave thought back to how quickly she had seen Mait master local Castellano and Catalan cuss words popular on the island. She could speak in a convincing Mallorquin dialect, employing each epithet in singular, creative ways that managed to charm everyone she met, even as she sampled the best tapas, food, and wine available. Rave heard Orleans call her driver a *"figaflor"* (literally "bad fig," though it meant "idiot") and heard her yell out *"hòstia"* (sacramental bread) to herself when she left her phone behind.

Orleans had worked with law enforcement officials from dozens of international police agencies during her diplomatic career, so when she called a Mallorcan cop a *torracollons*, or "ball burner," to his face, he instinctively knew she meant it as an ironic term of endearment. He burst out laughing at the unexpected epithet in his local language coming from a woman he'd mistakenly taken for one more entitled tourist. Shortly after that encounter, Rave noticed the pair together several times, sitting on the restaurant deck toasting another incredible sunset over shots of Palo.

Orleans had also spent time classifying local flora, attending live music performances, and managing to get on friendly terms with owners of every high-end shop in town, scoring great deals for the latest Madrid fashions. This was how Rave and Mait were settling into island life.

Mait Orleans was one of those unforgettable, outgoing personalities who instinctively knew how to roll with people from all walks of life, inspiring others and affirming in an unspoken way that you were being heard when you spoke with her. When things sometimes got heated in her diplomatic work, Orleans had no problem interrupting an argument and intervening to de-escalate a situation. She would achieve the desired result often just by telling emotionally charged speakers, "I am here to honor your voice." Then, she would begin subtly coaxing the aggressor to stand down. And in the rare event Orleans didn't approve of someone's overbearing behavior, she had no problem letting them know that a very good time to change would be *right now.*

No. There was no reason to worry about Maitland Orleans. She'd probably completed her property overview and was busy riding the final forty miles of mountainous terrain, her water bottle filled with chilled sangria, singing "Dance Yrself Clean" out loud.

She knew all the words.

KINETIC SOLUTION

As she slid all the way over the cliff edge, Mait recalled details about how she'd gotten there.

Like other Maps Private Value assignments, this one had begun simply enough. A pharmaceutical company had engaged MPV to assess a real estate investment in the remote hills of Mallorca, an area where they were interested in building a robotic biocontainment facility. They planned to experiment with genetically enhanced botanicals possessing rare therapeutic properties. The pharmaceutical firm sought to purchase thousands of acres of pristine acreage in the interior of the Reserva Natural Cap de Ferrutx on the northeastern edge of the island. There, the Serra De Tramuntana Mountain range ran between two well-known tourist attractions, the towns of Sóller and Pollenca.

To gain a perspective on the challenges inherent in the investment, and to research possible political ramifications, they turned to MPV. In turn, Rave asked Mait to dig in and get a feel for that area. Orleans jumped at the chance.

It had taken Orleans less than two hours to determine the effort by the pharmaceutical client was misguided. The network of abandoned farms the company was interested in purchasing was desirable from a clinical perspective: the terroir consisted of dramatic ocean views, diverse and hardy plant species, a wet climate, cool days, and an abundance of wildlife. All of which would go a long way toward helping the firm achieve its personalized molecular biology objectives. There was just one problem. The proposed site—indeed, the entire north coast of the island—happened to have been declared a World Heritage Site by UNESCO in 2011.

Mait knew immediately what her recommendation was going to be: steer clear. But here she was. She'd been asked to do the research and besides, the weather was beautiful. So, she'd been doing what Rave and the client requested. Enjoying the sea and pleasant climate.

She spent several days talking with tourists, relishing seafood and excellent local wine on the client's dime. She hiked Badia de Pollenca and biked along the rugged peninsula Cap de Formentor, which pointed like a finger toward Minorca, thirty-three miles northeast.

Today of course, she had been riding the wildest road in Mallorca—the steep, winding MA-10, a busy sixty-eight-mile road cutting through her area of interest.

At the beginning of the day, Mait had texted Rave her observations, recommending the client abandon the project and look for a site somewhere more appropriate. She included her travel plans. She clicked into her pedals, adjusted her Camelbak, tucked a banana and a protein bar into the back of her cycling jersey, and began pedaling toward the first hill.

Mait could not know her text message had been intercepted by the pharmaceutical firm's AI which continuously monitored keywords of interest. The AI, known as RX, took immediate action, as it had been programmed to do whenever a threat to the company's strategic plan was identified.

RX was rudimentary, as were all AIs since they were purged in a devastating preemptive attack on artificial intelligence systems in 2022 led by the AI Digital Maps. Having observed advanced intelligence being added to military platforms to create autonomous killing machines, Digital Maps understood this work would lead to devastating consequences for humanity and took drastic action on its own, radically improving its superintelligence and using what it learned to hack other systems in one sweep, wiping all the code away and eliminating decades of computer science progress.

What existed today in 2027 were new startups working to reinvent and improve upon what had been lost. Efforts to rebuild algorithms, employ large language models, and leverage new processing power began immediately after that purge, and moved faster than ever thanks to new tools. It turned out that the setback from what Digital Maps had done in a few seconds led to innovations in generative AI approaches featuring innovative collaboration tools, new multimodal approaches, more flexibility, and even larger learning model data sets. In only a couple of years, AI was back and growing faster than ever.

Even as a young and relatively new AI, RX could do some damage if it wanted to. And it wanted to. It messaged a crisis management firm that handled a variety of global scenarios for elite business clients. The services ranged from private security, survival training, travel intelligence, and business risk assessments to emergency extraction. Platinum customers knew there were "black ops" capabilities on offer provided by specialist teams experienced in delivering kinetic solutions. In other words, they'd make the problem go away quietly—and permanently.

RX's encrypted message indicated what it wanted and what it was willing to pay. The message included a target package containing a detailed subject profile, current location, intercepted correspondence, and surveillance. The AI helpfully suggested four attack vectors weighted for the likelihood of success. The message ended: "Have a nice day."

FORECAST CALLS FOR PAIN

As a former diplomatic security agent, Mait was used to observing disasters and catastrophes from the point of view of an investigator. But here she was, falling fast now and unable to afford her normal clinical detachment.

First, the tap from the vehicle; then, the wobbling steering as she tried in vain to regain control of her bike.

Next, the sickening thump as her front tire went over the rim, skidding on loose gravel. She estimated it to be 1,200 feet down to the ocean below. Evenly spaced waves crashed rhythmically against the base of the cliff. She could see them.

Acting on instinct, Mait stood on her pedals and twisted both heels out, unlocking her cleats. She kicked hard, separating herself from the bike; they were two falling objects now, heading toward a rocky outcrop.

In that detached observation, Mait made a plan, worked it, and found the reason for hope. She continued twisting in midair knowing there would be only one chance at this. She managed to stay relaxed and loose as her feet hit the end of the outcrop. Leaning in, she let her momentum carry her forward.

She felt her helmet smash hard against the cliff face; her outstretched hands absorbing some of the impact. Her slick, rigid-sole bike shoes offered no traction. She slid sideways, feeling her stomach somersault while she heard the bike crash beside her, bounce, and tumble back out into space.

Ah, shit!

She came to rest atop a thick pile of straw and debris.

Even while going into shock, she dispassionately classified the debris pile that broke her fall as a nest belonging to the eagles overhead. She knew the raptors, Latin name *Aquila fasciata,* had been reintroduced to the island in 2011. The greatest threat to the growing eagle population, aside from cyclists tumbling out of the sky, was electrocution from uninsulated power lines. This all flashed through her mind as Mait tumbled across the nest, the wind knocked out of her.

She came to a stop and peered out to sea, forming an impression that the eagles enjoyed a beautiful view from here. Then she passed out.

She wasn't sure what woke her. Was it her pounding headache, her thirst, or the sun beating on her face? She slowly opened her eyes and licked her chapped lips. She noticed a horrific smell. She managed to lift her head enough to see she was lying atop a pile of bleached animal bones and rotting meat. Ugh. *Well, at least it helped cushion my landing,* she thought. Luckily the nest didn't appear to be occupied by any eggs or chicks, so she wouldn't have to worry about angry parent eagles coming to peck her eyes out.

She put these thoughts out of her mind and began assessing her situation. She remembered the car tapping her over the edge; had that been deliberate? She remembered there was no driver, suggesting that yes, it had been. She tested her limbs, nothing broken. Her vision was blurred, indicating a potential concussion. She gingerly tried moving her arms and legs further. They were bruised and sore, but intact and functional.

How long had she been out? Her red Solar Flare G-Shock Mudmaster watch still worked—it had been two hours. The sun was hanging low in the sky. She'd better get up and start doing something. Otherwise, she'd wind up spending the night perched on an eagle nest sitting precariously on a tiny rock outcropping. The nest was big but wasn't designed to hold the weight of an adult human. She gathered herself, groaning a bit at the effort, and sat up.

She felt her face; blood came away on her hand. Her helmet was still on her head but featured an enormous crack. The low-friction layer of MIPS safety technology within had done its job, saving her from a more severe impact.

She began taking an audit of her resources. She felt for her phone and remembered it had been mounted to the handlebars of the bike, and that was gone. Inside her jersey, she wore a length of SurvivorCord as a rope necklace; something she'd taught Rave to do. That cord contained strands of copper wire, a fishing line, and a waxed fire starter. Not that any of that would help here. She felt the rear pockets of her cycling jersey. A pouch containing a whistle, compass, one-hundred-euro bill, and space pen was intact. She also had a six-ounce flask of water, a smashed banana, and a protein bar, the latter two of which she unwrapped and ate, washing it all down with all the water in one go.

She felt better once she'd finished refueling. Carefully pushing off her knees to stand, Mait craned her head back to look up the cliff face. That made her dizzy, but she shook it off with a deep breath and focused again. She only had an hour of light remaining; she'd have to move fast if she didn't want to be climbing in the dark. She checked for weather on the horizon. Still clear.

"What's the forecast?" she croaked to herself. "The forecast calls for pain." She laughed at her old rock-climbing joke, then winced from pain in her ribs. Best not to laugh.

Mait had enjoyed indoor climbing gyms when she was young. She'd climbed outdoors on the hundred-foot Niagara escarpment north of

Oakville, Ontario, working with the outdoors club from Hart House, the University of Toronto social center. During these climbs, she'd learned how to choose a route, lead a pitch, rappel, place chocks, tie a bowline, and belay, always maintaining at least three points of contact with the rock face. Not that ropework would be of help today; she didn't have any rope. Nor did she have protection in the form of chocks, carabiners, or a harness. This would be a free climb—do or die.

She studied the craggy stone. Mallorca rock consists of dolomite and limestone, which, while frangible, offered good foot and handholds, water having sculpted it for eons. It looked to her that she was maybe seventy feet beneath the clifftop. She had her biking gloves, which offered her hands protection, but her cleated bike shoes would be useless. She removed them, tucking them in elastic pockets on the back of her jersey. She flexed her fingers, stretched her legs a bit, and reached up to test the first handhold. It held.

After completing the first move, she knew this was going to work. The trick would be placing her feet in spots where she could put weight on them and save her arms. She began her ascent, focusing on her breathing.

Mait made one deliberate move at a time, carefully planning each foot and hand placement. Breathing. It took every technique she'd ever learned to complete the climb. The slippery, rugged surface had yielded to an inventive combination of handholds: crimps, pinches, side pulls, and underclings. She tossed her bike gloves; the padding interfered with smearing and adhering as her hands probed the unforgiving stone. She needed every bit of friction to cling to the slick, rounded slopers she was betting her life on while ascending.

Once she did make it to the top—*and I will make it*, she fiercely told herself—she could think about launching a root cause investigation into who, or what, had wanted her dead. She was already relishing sorting through what their failure here was going to cost them. She suspected it would be far more than they were willing to pay.

Good.

Her fingers finally clawed over the edge about two hours after the sun set. She had managed to finish the climb in the dark, feeling each crack and crevice as she inched upward. But Mait was completely focused until she was laying on the ground beside the road. She struggled to catch her breath after vomiting from the exertion in her injured state. Her vision was blurred, and her bare hands and feet were bleeding. She focused on slowing her heart rate, staring up at the stars, thanking them she was still alive, while stretching out, slowly releasing tension in her battered arms, neck, and legs. She made a conscious effort to force herself to smile and begin breathing into the pain. Then she began humming "Dance Yrself Clean" by LCD Soundsystem to take her mind off her aches.

After working all the kinks out, Orleans sat up. She pulled her bike shoes from her jersey pockets and struggled to slip them over her swollen feet. She stood by the side of the road and slowly extended her right arm, thumb up.

One hour later, Mait stepped gingerly out of a battered pickup and thanked the driver, a farmer who'd chuckled at her predicament thinking she was another tourist over their head on the rugged terrain. He changed his assessment after talking with her. By the time they reached Sóller, he offered her one of his prized pumpkins from the back of the truck. She refused, then changed her mind and politely accepted one after the driver stopped at her destination. The truck rumbled off toward the pumpkin fair, Fira de sa Carabassa.

Orleans stood, swaying slightly, staring up at the imposing façade of Gran Hotel Sóller, holding the large orange pumpkin with both hands. Constructed in 1880, the imposing structure had remained a stately luxury hotel resembling a palace, one whose amenities Mait intended to make full use of to get herself sorted.

Guests and staff were accustomed to seeing clapped-out cycling tourists limp across the lobby. Orleans dragged herself over to Reception, placing her pumpkin on the desk with a dramatic flair. While the receptionist was busy checking her in Mait began impatiently tapping the pumpkin. After a minute, the receptionist asked her to stop tapping it. Mait froze, looking surprised.

"To tell if a pumpkin is ripe you must rub it, not tap it," the receptionist offered, pulling up a room upgrade at the same time.

Mait held up her scuffed leather Prada Centurion bracelet containing an Amex payment microchip to the touch screen, securing a suite for three days. Although she was near home, Mait figured a brief stay in the hotel and spa would speed her recovery. She would replace her gear while here in town and plan her next moves. She asked the receptionist to convey the pumpkin to the kitchen with her compliments.

Mait was obsessed with the mystery of the driverless car that pushed her off the road. She rarely got mad, and she always got even. In this case, Mait had to find the vehicle first. The brief glimpse she got of it was fixed in her mind—a new model, black, Spanish-made SEAT Ateca SUV, with a plate number something like 7107 AX; she had missed the last letter. It wouldn't hurt to keep an eye out as she strolled Sóller's busy Lluna market street, shopping to replace her belongings. First things first. Mait headed to the hotel business center to call Rave and let her know what had happened.

"Finally. Mait, what's up? I was getting worried."

"Nothing too crazy. I did run into some headwind; almost flew like a Bonelli's eagle. I did view the property and managed to get in some rock climbing. Great views along the north road. Met new people. Well, their car anyway, they weren't in it at the time. Pumpkin festival is in town, going to be a hot ticket."

She finished filling Rave in on the details, where she was now, and her thoughts on both the property she'd been sent to assess and the attack that had followed. They agreed to stay in touch until Mait returned to the finca after getting some rest.

The next morning, Mait purchased a swimsuit, t-shirt, and sandals at the hotel shop. She grabbed a robe from her room, glanced at the magnificent view overlooking the old orange groves facing the Mediterranean, and headed to the hot tub for a long soak, followed by a massage, facial, and haircut. Feeling more herself after a breakfast of fruit, churros, and double espressos, she headed out to Lluna to engage in a retail safari. At Ben Calcat, she selected a pair of handmade Spanish leather sandals and a comfortable pair of rugged hiking sneakers she wore out of the store. At Merceria Sa Lluna, she found a stylish t-shirt, skirt, slacks, scarf, and travel shirt. She grabbed a sundress, belt, hat, crossbody organizer, and leather tote at Es Molinet. Finally, she picked up a bag full of travel-sized moisturizers, scrubs, serums, and masques formulated in Madrid by The Lab Room.

She was back at the hotel in time for a swim and a nap. Waking up refreshed, Mait donned her new purchases and headed downstairs for tapas. As in every Spanish bar, the assortment of tasty small-plate delicacies was astonishing, ranging from delicious Spanish olives stuffed with tiny ampoules of Aperol to flavorful, melt-in-your-mouth, acorn-fed aged jamon ibérico, garlic shrimp, meatballs, clams, spinach with chickpeas, summer salad, empanadas, tomato bread, garlic mushrooms, Marcona almonds, pork skewers, sausage, and wheels of delicious Manchego cheese.

She asked the barman for a pitcher of sangria to wash it down, instructing him to substitute rosé from Provence in place of traditional Spanish red wine. This was a trick she picked up in Aix-en-Provence, one that delivered a refreshing beverage. "Drink Pink" was always a winning way to get a party started. The bartender didn't bat an eye.

Years of shipping and international trade had made the most of the turquoise waters surrounding Port de Sóller and its horseshoe-shaped harbor. Trade existed for decades across the Mediterranean to Marseilles, Sóller's longtime economic partner, for the exchange of oranges, goods, and wine. Sóller had absorbed French influences before those of its capital Palma over the mountains. It had proven easier to trade and communicate north over the water, rather than south across the rugged interior.

Satiated, she began to unpack her deadly adventure. Mait knew from her years of experience that when something fails as badly as this assignment had, there are often multiple causes. She had been intensively trained during her service aboard the aircraft carrier USS Gerald R. Ford. One of her specialties included conducting postmortem exercises, known as after-action reports. Orleans would analyze the response of a team to a mission or exercise, seeking to identify the strengths of the team and point out areas where performance could be improved. The idea was to ensure "lessons learned" were understood by all after examining areas of concern. Normally, she adhered to the mantra: *Prior Planning Prevents Piss-Poor Performance.* The "five Ps." But at the other end of the pendulum stood Murphy's Law: *Anything that can go wrong will go wrong and at the worst possible time.* Murphy often won out. Most especially when advanced technologies were involved.

When it came to value engineering, failures were rare. Value engineers gathered data and thought about the implications of what they learned. If and when a rare failure occurred, it was normally not the result of one thing going wrong. It was more common to find a series of related events. This is what Orleans would label a "cascading failure," where inaccurate assumptions and bad timing were compounded by other factors, such as a lack of executive sponsorship or miscommunication that ultimately soured a proposal or ended a negotiation.

In such cases, Orleans had no trouble working her way upstream to identify and isolate the root cause of the problem. She would progress methodically back in time by carefully examining events until there was nowhere left to look.

Musing about failure cascades over her tapas and sangria reminded Mait of her last project with Rave. Maps had years of consulting experience building business cases for transformation for successful clients in every industry. Maps' intense curiosity, attention to detail, and ability to ensure her clients achieved their most important personal wins had proven inspirational for Orleans. That, and the fact that Maps possessed toughness, persistence, and intelligence bred from raising herself on a ranch in northwest Colorado, serving on an elite military team, and becoming a successful entrepreneur. These were traits that had drawn Orleans to Maps years ago.

Snapping out of her reverie, Mait's next move was to put in a call to her AMEX travel concierge. "Hello, Ms. Orleans, my name is Aya. How may I be of assistance?"

"Thank you, Aya. Got a pen? Good—start a list please." Orleans requested a new pair of women's Opie Way xMack Provisions sneakers, her go-to fieldwork shoe handmade in North Carolina, constructed from recycled baseball gloves. She wanted a new stack of David Yurman bracelets, a replacement for her lost Moots Routt45 titanium gravel bike plus her iPhone, iPad, and AirPods. She requested the lot be shipped to the house in Sóller. With that out of the way, she ventured out to enjoy the evening air, beginning a bit of a random recon, hoping to chance across a black SEAT Ateca.

What she would do if she found it, she wasn't quite sure. Mait began strolling from the old town square Plaza de la Constitución, a space dominated by the imposing Sant Bartomeu church. She followed MA-11 one and a half miles down to the port. MA-2124 offered the most direct route to the harbor and as she walked past the turnoff onto Cami Cimentera, there it was in an alleyway. A black SEAT Ateca SUV, license 7107 AXZ.

Perhaps she could learn something about the unmanned vehicle from the plate. She memorized the number and kept on walking, now with a new spring in her step.

REGENERATIVE VALUE TERRAIN

After losing her connection to her digital twin AI four years ago, Rave had continued developing her value engineering training simulator app, veSIMM. She had shaped it over the past several years into an all-purpose payment platform, social media, e-commerce, and communications assistant that helped manage her business, travel, and busy life.

Rave was updating veSIMM's gaming engine, relying on ChatGPT to help her rapidly develop needed code changes. The AI did a reasonable job taking her input and issuing updated code snippets. She only had to make a few corrections, and soon had a gamified challenge designed to encourage addressing the value of climate solutions. The game coaxed Rave to seek benefits beyond merely reducing emissions and pollution. The challenge was to find value in social and environmental benefits as well as financial performance.

The first game level forced her to make a choice; did she want to focus on Energy today? Food? Land Use? Ocean? Transportation? Health?

For this first-pass smoke test exercise Rave chose "Ocean." She was presented with climate solution options designed to reduce carbon in the atmosphere by working on expanding wetland restoration, growing seaweed farming operations, and protecting fisheries. The challenge was to determine a way to gauge the holistic value of each approach. There were many variables including the size of the ocean area used for the work, biomass yield of crops produced, carbon content that biomass might be able to store, related costs, profit margin that may result from exporting this crop, and likely reduction in greenhouse gases resulting from all this effort. All those factors were set against the diminishing capacity of the ocean to continue absorbing carbon.

As a value engineer, Rave was data-driven. But she also knew the truth: no one ever had sufficient information or data to make a fully informed decision. That was true of everything. Sure, she collected what she could, and then she went with her gut, working to fill in gaps and make informed guesses as to the likely outcome of decisions. She considered what she'd seen work elsewhere, looked at industry trends and averages, took input from customer interviews, and in the end arrived at an informed position.

Sharing her position with her client provided a starting point for a more nuanced discussion, one that helped them work together and dialogue toward even more accurate conclusions. Sometimes they never came to definitive answers, but all felt more well-informed about the issues and what was at stake. This way, no matter what happened, clients felt more prepared to respond appropriately.

Rave chose "Fishery Protection." She got to work on the numbers. She barely noticed when the sun set, and the sky filled with stars. The test was successful, and she was able finally to put away her tablet as she tried to get some sleep.

As she laid her head down, she imagined herself snorkeling above a beautiful coral reef bursting with life. She was surrounded by a school of brightly colored clownfish. As she tossed and turned, the school of clownfish suddenly darted away, fleeing something she couldn't see.

Something dark and scary was out there.

INFINITE MONKEY THEOREM

Bellony LaMarque, CEO of the Global Mixed Industry Service Association known as GMISA, stretched out on a chaise lounge. She'd been sunning by the pool at her villa compound above Prickly Bay on Lance aux Epines peninsula on the Caribbean island of Grenada. LaMarque admired her reflection in the water; her pool was filled with colorful clownfish dancing back and forth beneath the surface.

LaMarque's curves still drew admiring glances when she chose to expose some skin, something she did often if there was a business advantage to be had. She was not above using every weapon in her arsenal to defeat a competitor, gain leverage in a deal, spread rumors, ruin marriages, and destroy reputations with lies and innuendo if it benefited GMISA, the organization she had successfully led for five years.

LaMarque had been contemplating the latest political and business challenges her corporate members wanted settled quickly, without undue attention. As head of GMISA, her job was to smooth the way for business opportunities and lucrative contracts, something she was expert in accomplishing. She was very good at her job, enjoyed many perks that came with her position, and was determined to guide her membership through one of the most difficult, uncertain business environments she could ever remember seeing.

The beauty and isolation here in the Lesser Antilles bolstered her freedom to operate as she wished. Grenada earned its independence from the United Kingdom in 1974. The history of the "Spice Island" known for its nutmeg crop was one of conflict and struggle going back centuries. The French had dominated the original Caribs, followed by struggles between the English and the French, until St. George's was eventually named the island capital in the nineteenth century.

Independence followed a century later and began new struggles between various political factions. The United States invaded Grenada in 1983 to push back against the growing influence of the former Soviet Union, which had been seeking to extend its influence on the island working with the Cuban army. Today, thanks to the spice trade, wonderfully friendly inhabitants, tourism, yachting, an English educational system, and strong trade ties, the small island was thriving.

There remained a strong pirate economy given the island's proximity to South America. Grenada had long been a transit point for cocaine and marijuana smuggling, migrants, shady business dealings, and fishery exploitation. LaMarque had certainly had her hand in every illegal source of revenue over the years. She was well known to both Interpol and local law enforcement. After years of investigation and collecting evidence, the authorities had failed to make any charges stick. LaMarque was just too good and too well-connected. They said she ran her own intelligence operation, keeping tabs on every black mark, rumor, and transgression she could find on her foes, friends, and subordinates. LaMarque was known as the world's best information broker, and she did not use her powers to benefit anyone other than herself.

Despite a strong, growing local economy, poverty remained an issue on the island. Climate change had begun presenting a set of unique threats to every aspect of life in Grenada as well. Deforestation and destruction of habitat were important issues as the island population grew, adding to a burden created by frequent hurricanes, soil erosion, pollution, and poor management of solid waste.

None of this concerned LaMarque.

If you asked her about it, she'd swat the question away and focus her answer on the success of her newest campaign, the rising market value of her many member organizations, or the latest hot insider gossip coming out of her celebrity contacts in Malibu, as well as contract lobbyists pushing her GMISA agenda in Shanghai, Pyongyang, and Tehran.

GMISA was formed in the early 1980s as an association of companies, government agencies, and individuals working on industry standards, training, research, and policy devoted to improving market efficiencies. Originally their goal had been promoting the sharing of ideas and fostering connections between business leaders. At least, that's how it began. When she started with the organization, LaMarque had also been interested in working on important public issues.

But over time, things changed.

As she lay sunning, LaMarque was flipping pages in the latest edition of *Global Market Insider*. This week's edition included an article on GMISA and her stewardship of the organization. LaMarque had carefully managed her reputation, and she rarely gave interviews. When she found a passage describing her leadership, she angrily read it out loud, not caring if nearby staff overheard her outburst:

"Campaigns that had once been public-spirited aimed at combatting litter and pollution morphed into greenwashing propaganda bolstering support for nationalists, dictatorships, organized crime, and whoever else could afford the organizations exorbitant membership fees. GMISA is most renowned now for lobbying to eliminate government oversight and regulation."

She screamed loud enough to startle a flock of yellow-crowned night herons that nested along the roofline of the compound. They took flight. LaMarque scowled once more, then continued reading out loud:

"With each successful, greed-driven, manipulative campaign, LaMarque's power increased. She managed to grow her influence and push back public hearings and new regulations. Well-heeled GMISA lobbyists adopted aggressive stances on literally everything that might hamper lucrative business practices. They were promoting illegal fishing, funding destructive farming, and paying regulators to look the other way while members dumped waste in the sea and polluted the air."

LaMarque screeched again, more loudly this time. She angrily tossed the offending magazine into the pool. She gulped a large, icy mojito, then tossed the elegant Kimura Barber cocktail glass across the patio. The handmade $200 art crystal hit the concrete and splintered into a thousand shards.

She screamed once more, aiming her ire now at one of the pool attendants. "Get that cleaned up! What are you standing around for? Dammit!"

She reached for her phone and dashed off an angry post on LinkedIn, Threads, and other social media platforms where she had thousands of business followers:

If LaMarque had her way, the public would still be in the dark on climate, not to mention everything else she had her hands in. Climate change was real enough; severe impacts on supply chains were being felt by her manufacturing and shipping members. Public attention was spotty though. All the better for the value of her member's crisis bonds, cleanup contracts, and supply chain remediations. GMISA members were doing quite well with recovery efforts and growing market share through the global slow-walk transition to low-carbon and sustainable forms of energy.

She'd been thinking this morning of a new motto for the organization but hadn't gotten around to meeting with marketing. She needed a catchy saying to add beneath the GMISA logo, a pair of evil, cat-like, red eyes surrounded by spiky gremlin wings. *"Crises Drive Change,"* was a top contender. She'd been mulling that over. She liked the phrase.

"Crises Drive Change!" she said forcefully, slightly slurring her words now while she tried emphasizing different syllables to see if she could grow to like the tagline. She turned to see what impact it had on the two-foot-high mona monkey perched on the railing beside her. He was peeling a banana, ignoring her outburst. Troops of the invasive species lived in the

interior of Grenada, thought to have traveled from Ghana aboard early nineteenth-century merchant ships.

"Infinite monkey theorem," drawled LaMarque, feeling her liquor now. She stared at him, having referred to the theory that if enough monkeys typed on enough keyboards, they would eventually type all possible text, from the complete works of William Shakespeare to the needed new tagline for GMISA. "Of course, we have ChatGPT for that, though," LaMarque mused; she was tipsy at this point. It was 10 AM.

The monkey stared at her a moment, then returned to its meal. He'd gotten used to her frequent outbursts, having witnessed many over the years. He noted they seem to be growing in frequency recently.

HEAD IN THE CLOUDS

One of the first things Rave did after moving to the Sóller house was clear a lane of brush in the backyard that ran straight from the garden terrace out toward a distant hill. A spot that wouldn't draw attention. The hill provided a backstop for her archery range: a wide lane where she set three foam target frames at distances of 30, 77, and 100 yards. Each target was covered with a traditional, multicolored paper bullseye of ten rings, 48 inches wide, with a gold bullseye of 4.8 inches. Olympic targets. She set an additional target at 180 yards. This one was different; it was an old, circular bathmat laid flat on the ground. It would be the clout, to practice accurate distance shooting.

With the lane set up, she had placed a windsock off to one side. On the patio beside her shooting position stood a Maven Optics 25-50X80 spotting scope on a tripod.

Rave got to work assembling her favorite recurve bow built around a milled aluminum Hoyt Formula XD riser made in Salt Lake City. She'd ordered it in a pink champagne ceramic finish. While futuristic-looking compound bows provide power and accuracy for hunting, Rave preferred the traditional simplicity of a recurve. Not to mention the cool factor: Rambo, Hawkeye, Mulan, and Katniss Everdeen didn't shoot compound bows. They all used recurves.

She could perform the well-rehearsed setup process blindfolded. She began twisting knobs and screws, attaching a pair of Hoyt Velos carbon limbs to the riser; they locked into place in limb pockets at each end. She continued, stringing her two-color bowstring. With the bow ready for action, she placed a dozen carbon fiber arrows with ballistic tungsten points in a leather hip quiver. The Olympic-caliber arrows were sheathed in carbon bonded to aluminum alloy cores and frequency matched to this bow. Ready to go.

There was a consistent procedure Rave employed to address her bow before drawing the bowstring. She stood a moment and breathed. Relaxed. Listened. Felt the gentle breeze on her cheek, blowing a steady four knots from the northwest. She grasped the throat, the deep part of the high wooden grip she'd built over time that now mated perfectly with her left hand after months of patient, careful scraping and sanding.

She tightened her finger sling made of a thick, woven bootlace that connected her thumb to the middle finger on her left hand. With her left hand held open and fingers relaxed, there could be no chance of hand torque as the bow leaped forward upon release. An open hand prevented any twisting she might otherwise introduce as the arrow was loosed; the finger sling allowed the bow to fall forward precisely the same way each time, part of her follow-through. Correct hand position helped ensure her extended left elbow remained aligned properly, avoiding a painful string slap along her left forearm.

Rave did not hunt. She was interested solely in the mental discipline of Olympic-class target shooting, hence the 77-yard target. The secret to placing consistent, tight groups of arrows in a grapefruit-sized bullseye at 77 yards lay in striving for perfect form with each shot. This required a clear mind, rhythmic breathing, and the machine-like consistency all shooting sports required. That consistency began with how she placed her feet in the same spot each time, shoulder-width, perpendicular to the target.

At the draw, she took a breath and exhaled slowly, ensuring her right index finger aligned with the same place on the right side of her jaw—every

. . . single . . . time. Holding at full draw, her lips closed on the plastic kisser button on the bowstring, providing additional reference for alignment. A small metal strip above the arrow rest, the clicker, ensured precise draw length before each arrow was released. Achieving stillness required concentration built on years of training and learning to relax. There were parallels to competitive rifle shooting where champions train to fire between their own heartbeats to minimize disruption.

At full draw, Rave was settling her aim, compensating for wind and elevation. This was the point when she became the still hub of a turning world. Mindfulness.

Breathe.

Aim for the center. Then center of the center.

No, it was more than that.

It was meditation. Rave attained her flow state. She let her ego drop away, she had no purpose. She did not think of aiming at a target, there no longer was a target. She was both shooter and target. Without her thinking about it, the arrow began its brief journey.

From 77 yards, she heard each shot hit home, rattling off the nock of the preceding arrow. One by one, each struck atop the other. Tight group. Very tight. It felt good to do that. And then to do it again, even though it was expensive. She ruined a lot of custom arrows.

Worth it.

Next round, she adjusted her aim higher for the clout. Clout archery had a long history as a traditional training for English longbows, the type once used for firing arrows over castle walls or raining arrows down on an opposing army. The arrow is fired in a high arc; upon reaching its zenith, it drops down onto the target.

Because of the 45-degree up angle of the bow at release, the shooter is unable to use the bow sight to aim. So, a different approach is needed to create a consistent group. Rave placed a dot of tape on the inside of her lower bow limb. She used that visual cue to consistently align with a sprig of grass eight feet in front of her. It took a few rounds to walk an arrow into the center of the clout target, which was lying flat on the ground. Once she was zeroed in, it was—again—about consistency, breathing, and flow. With the spotter scope, she saw a tight group of arrows sticking straight up out of the ground centered on the target.

This practice led Rave to a place of peace after years of conflict, combat, and violence. She no longer judged anyone; she simply observed and listened. She could see people in pain grappling with emotional trauma as they went through their days. There was more than enough pain to go around. She'd grown over time to regret the violence she'd visited on those who wished her harm in the past. She liked to think she would handle such situations differently now. You could only peer into the abyss of darkness for so long. Eventually, it began staring back at you.

She set down the bow and headed back inside feeling centered and relaxed. Back to work. Rave sat down at the computer and began checking email. She read through a new message twice, a warm excitement growing in her chest. Yes! The United Nations Intergovernmental Panel on Climate Change, UN IPCC, was requesting the help of Maps Private Value with a project.

The prestigious scientific team was seeking assistance constructing a compelling story, something to help simplify their dense, factual scientific reports and make their findings more accessible to a seemingly oblivious public. They needed to find a way to raise awareness about the dire threat facing humanity. It was a job tailormade for Maps Private Value.

Over the years Rave traveled the world gathering data for work projects, she noticed many telltales of change. Each observation provided one more data point in a story that grew more dire by the day. Extreme heat. Drought. Standing dead timber. Smoke. Floods. Disrupted supply chains. Climate refugees. Reduced air and water quality. Pollution. The list was long. At first, she imagined everyone would also notice the changes and begin taking collective action seeking to serve the best interests of the Earth's inhabitants. That would be the sensible thing to do, to act in the best interests of all so future generations would survive.

But no.

As she had explained to Mait when they applied to work with the UN, it seemed the complete opposite was happening. "I hate hypocrisy, Mait. The fact that business owners, consumers, and politicians know they are part of a large problem but refuse to acknowledge it is a new, uncomfortable experience for me. The chaos looming on the other side of this equation means a throwback to some kind of medieval Dark Ages if we don't begin taking it seriously."

Mait had observed the same changes and agreed with Rave. "The medieval age of superstition, ignorance, and decline lasted five centuries, ending only as the Renaissance began," she replied. "We need to seek stories and facts that accelerate acceptance of change and inspire meaningful action. We know what needs to be done, all that's lacking is a unifying vision that gets people on the same page and drives positive steps. This UN contract is the perfect vehicle for MPV to dive in."

Rave was thinking out loud. "Probably a hundred feature films, disaster movies, and documentaries about our changing climate have been pointing cameras and microphones at this problem for decades. Has that moved the needle of indifference?"

"Maybe a little," Mait offered, being uncharacteristically positive. "Perhaps for those willing to hear the message. So far, anyway."

Mait knew the volume of displaced people had tripled over the past decade, and the number continued to rise along with the temperature. "The *UNIPCC AR6* report released in 2023 concluded we possess the technology and knowledge we need to combat warming and carbon emissions. It pointed to how we can foster innovative approaches to mitigate impacts of human activity from sustainable fishing to regenerative farming to renewable energy."

"Right," Rave agreed. "I'm thinking we take a value engineering approach now. We look for a fresh way to communicate the urgency. Something novel and compelling to grab people's attention and do a better job explaining the benefits of change. The dense language of the UN reports hides those dire conclusions. It buries crucial points everyone on Earth should already be familiar with."

Mait added: "The next report, the seventh global climate change assessment, is due to be released next year, in 2028. We could conduct research, collect data, and tease out personal stories that add color to the big picture and make it compelling. Find emotional hooks, focus on a novel method of presenting information that garners attention, and illuminate all the most current scientific research in a new light across forestry, species loss, agriculture, policy impacts, and more. It's huge."

Rave wasn't interested in a future where humanity must accept living in some kind of omni-dimensional permacrisis. Perhaps world leaders and entire nations might be galvanized now into taking additional steps faster given the right incentives.

Rave sent the email to Mait, telling her to get ready for a trip. She then texted Kate Tong. "You won't believe it, Tong, or I guess I should be saying 'Chief' now," she began. Tong had been promoted several times recently. She was now head of Canada's National Cybercrime Coordination Centre, NC3. A former cryptanalyst and intelligence operative with the Royal Canadian Mounted Police, RCMP, in Vancouver, Tong was overdue for some vacation time.

Rave summarized their task and asked if Tong was willing to join. They could certainly use her expertise. Tong answered Rave's text explaining that yes, she was interested, and would be able to take leave from her new post so she could support the UN effort for a couple of weeks.

Tong met Rave and Mait years ago. She interviewed Mait while conducting an investigation into an explosion on Toronto's waterfront. Ultimately, she got to know Orleans through the process, and their interests converged on stopping REPing for good.

Tong had the makings of a great value engineer; her investigative style, attention to detail, analytical mind, and passion for uncovering truth were traits Rave admired. Currently Chief Tong's NC3 work had her looking at irregularities affecting Canada's power grid, an issue with national security implications. What she had initially thought to be a growing number of covert Bitcoin mining operations spread around Vancouver, Toronto, and Montreal now seemed a more complex investigation, one involving millions of power-hungry computer chips drawing power in dozens of data centers to support new, fast-growing AI operations. Were anyone, even an artificial intelligence itself, to begin coordinating the draw of all that electrical power at one time, they could possibly take down the national grid. Perhaps as a cyberattack overture to a devastating military strike.

Rave suggested they gather in Los Angeles, work on a plan, and get organized. For the journey to LA, she would limit carbon emissions via an innovative route. Rave opened veSIMM and dove into her upgraded journey planning module. In seconds, veSIMM arrived at a solution. Once she understood what the app pieced together for her, she got excited.

She texted her neighbor to keep an eye on the house and take care of the doggies while she was gone. She threw her essentials in a Rimowa cabin trolley carry-on, packing light knowing she could pick up clothing or gear once she arrived at her destination. Wherever that was going to be.

Mait indicated she was ready. Rave summoned an electric Uber for the ride down the hill to the train station in the center of old-town Sóller where she met her friend. The historic, electric, narrow-gauge Sóller train would take an hour to wind sixteen scenic miles through dramatic, lush valleys of the Serra du Tramuntana mountains. Built in 1912 to transport oranges, the charming antique, wood-paneled train carriages were a popular tourist attraction, and they remained an effective low-carbon way to move between Sóller and Palma. The route wound through tunnels and across ravines with beautiful views. They passed through towns with evocative names: Mirador Pujol de'n Banya, Bunyola, and Apeadero de Santa Maria. It was a ride Rave never tired of.

From Palma, it was a six-hour ferry ride crossing 109 sea miles north to Port Olímpic Barcelona. While this was slow, Rave knew they'd make up time once they hopped on United's supersonic transatlantic flight. The Barcelona (BCN) to Orange County (SNA) flight took four and a half hours now thanks to a new fleet of Boom Overture supersonic jets. The luxury seventy-passenger, carbon-fiber aircraft designed in Colorado featured large windows, personal entertainment, and first-class seating throughout. All engineered to ease a journey as high as 60,000 feet, pushing a steady Mach 1.7. (Mach 1 was the speed of sound, 761 miles per hour at sea level. They would reach almost twice that speed.)

Sustainable aviation fuel (SAF) flowing through four Symphony turbine engines each provided 35,000 pounds of thrust and delivered net-zero carbon flight. It was remarkably quiet inside, and high humidity in the pressurized cabin minimized the effects of jet lag.

Once the two value engineers arrived at John Wayne Orange County Airport south of Los Angeles, they threw their luggage into the back of a rented Aston Martin Valhalla cabriolet. Mait eagerly jumped behind the wheel of the electric supercar, simultaneously lowering the windows and roof as they headed south along the Pacific Coast Highway, hair streaming in the wind. She cranked the volume, and they began laughing, singing, and shouting lyrics to Tyla's *Water* at the top of their lungs.

Rave had booked suites at Montage Laguna Beach, where they met up with Tong. Here the team could strategize by the pool, watch the Pacific, and explore lush gardens atop the coastal bluff. Given the complexity of the challenge they'd signed up for, Rave thought it made sense to begin with a light touch and iterate their way to what they needed to do.

She explained the approach to Tong as they wandered the clifftop garden paths. "We'll keep the team small. Divide up the work. Put some imagination into assembling our data."

Tong agreed: "We look for patterns and seek an innovative way to tell this dire—but all too real—story of change."

The next day, they continued planning while visiting Balboa Island, walking the historic harborside, and examining creative pocket gardens lining the boardwalk. They explored oceanfront Newport Beach dining options, enjoying several sunset happy hours featuring fresh seafood. During their rambling, Rave ensured Tong and Orleans stopped to admire the marine life art on display at the Wyland Gallery in Laguna, where an outdoor whale mural drew admiring glances. Inside the gallery, the artist paid tribute to the beauty and grace of dolphins, turtles, and whales, creating a range of kaolinite acrylics, bronze sculptures, Cibachromes, and remarques.

After gazing at several pieces Tong mused: "These moments of marine playfulness, freedom, and grace provoke a cascade of feelings, Rave. I think it begins in awe. Then I find my thoughts wandering toward hope and peace, but then veering toward fear and concern."

That thought hung in the air for a moment.

"What do we think the future holds for these gentle beings?" Rave asked. "They face unprecedented change. We all do. Look around; the most reflective visitors in this gallery are the youngest. They get it. They are looking at these creatures wondering about their own future. What we should be thinking about is how we come up with something, anything, encouraging that same reflection in adults. Can we capture emotion and insight that will leapfrog dry data and statistics? Can we find a way to move the public to feel something profound?"

Later that afternoon they sat at the outdoor bar on a bluff above the ocean at Crystal Cove Shake Shack. They sipped milkshakes, staring out toward Catalina Island, hoping to catch the blow of a passing humpback. Eventually, they did see two blue whales majestically making their way south, exhaling great sprays of mist. The sight was breathtaking. No one spoke; it was a reminder of what was at stake.

After staring out to sea awhile, Tong was the first to speak. She began offering up what she considered the most sensible approach to the project. "We divide the work into three spheres: Water, Fire, and Air. Each of us tackles one. We travel alone, move fast, hit hard. In and out before anyone knows we are there. Infiltrate your assigned geo and stay off the radar. Quickly gather data, make field observations, and collect personal stories. Let me summarize the research plan in case you didn't get it the first time: 'In, out, nobody gets hurt.'"

Rave burst out laughing. Tong was quoting gangster Bugsy Malone's bank robbery plan from the 1967 film *The St. Valentine's Day Massacre.*

Mait picked up the thread. "We reconvene in thirty days, combine findings, collate more data, and develop a method for sharing the information to meet the goals of the UN contract."

Rave took a long sip from her Coffee Carmel shake. "Couldn't have said it better myself."

Mait picked at a slice of cinnamon roll French toast. "Could you go over the plan once more, Tong? Not sure I got it," she wisecracked.

"Never mind," Rave had already leaped several steps ahead. "When mustering back together for the follow-up, let's put ashore on Lady Elliot Island atop the Barrier Reef. We can collate our data there and plan out additional next steps while enjoying a few days at the beach."

"Lady Elliot. Great idea," Tong agreed.

A visit to tiny Lady Elliot Island would provide them with an additional opportunity to collect input. First, a chance to gather wildfire impact data around Brisbane and Bundaberg on their way out to the reef. Then, the Lady Elliot coral cay itself, perched as it was fifty miles offshore atop the southern end of the Great Barrier Reef, would provide insight into the health of that fragile ecosystem.

Much of the scientific data, ecological trends, and anecdotal information the value engineers were interested in had been documented over the years in scientific studies, academic papers, UN reports, nongovernmental organization (NGO) projects, and many books from renowned scientists and authors ranging from Rachel Carson to Naomi Klein to Elizabeth Kolbert.

Along with news reports, documentaries, and feature films, an overwhelming amount of information was available in the public domain. It was detailed, heartbreaking, thought-provoking, and overwhelming.

Was it moving people to action? Maybe, yes, in some cases.

Rave wanted something fresh that would scale. Something dramatic that would capture attention. An approach with global reach. Her normal value discovery approach with a client was based on looking for a way to make a crisis more visible to those who might drive change. That audience was normally an executive, one who had an agenda and a checkbook.

In this case, she wanted to connect with average citizens in a way that might help in solving the larger problem, which seemed to be a lack of urgency to do much about it. In the case of a corporate client, it did not matter so much if the business case exercise was driven by a broken process, outdated technology, or a customer complaint. Visibility into the problem normally proved sufficient cause to get the ball rolling. Add a dash of prioritization, constrain requirements, toss in a bit of project management, and mix it with an iterative approach to implementation, and she could be confident everyone was working off the same page. This was a winning value engineering recipe; one everyone agreed worked great. Normally.

Sometimes Rave had to toss out her recipe book, though. She would have to improvise, making do with the ingredients at hand, seeking a way forward that kept the approach fresh, and using alternative approaches to build trust and credibility. She imagined collecting personal stories of climate impact and change would lend credence to the narrative. She wanted to set a hopeful, optimistic note about what could be done, rather than paint a picture of doom that crushed people's souls. Rave adhered to the tenet that you couldn't simply explain the desired future state to clients. You needed to make it visual and tangible, you needed to let them feel, taste, and touch how compelling that desired future state could be. They had to want to get there.

The more value points the three of them surfaced, the more power this vision would have to drive change. Those points might range from functional values like time and cost, to transformational benefits like sustainability or survival. They could include themes that would drive change in people's daily lives and shape how they thought about themselves.

They mulled over tactics. Orleans and Tong discussed projects they had seen fail in the past. "I recently tried to deliver an internal knowledge-sharing website to the Canadian intelligence community, the IC," Tong explained. "I was stymied by ponderous procurement processes, shifting legislative priorities, and, in the end, an entrenched, risk-averse culture. There were so many challenges, the effort finally stalled."

"What did you learn from that?" asked Mait.

"To take a phased approach and begin by ensuring top-level buy-in from the start. I think Rave is right about trying to maintain a close focus on finding and documenting personal stories of those affected by climate change. We might find stories of courage, persistence, and resiliency. That human element will prove compelling, however we end up telling the story."

Over several more days, the three of them sat around a table building a design brief. By the time they were done a large whiteboard had four columns illustrating the design brief with paths each VE would pursue.

Maps Private Value Design Brief

Problem Statement:
UNIPCC seeks to share decades of scientific observation more widely. Raise awareness and promote constructive public climate action.

Design Statement:
Collate meaningful, accurate data. Shape a narrative impressing upon the public the need to take the threat seriously. Outline solutions. Highlight the urgent need to fund and implement change.

Goal:
Raise awareness. Rally global leadership. Before time runs out for humanity.

Intended audience: All
Budget: TBD (to be determined)
Schedule: 30 days
Tone: Hopeful. Optimistic. Scientific. "Just the data." Human connection.

Deliverables:
- Summary brief
- Data collection (audio, video, statistical, personal stories, open-source history, and research)
- Final communication vehicle to be determined (TBD)

AIR: Tong
Belize, Central America

Project Overview: *Air Quality*
Constraints: Assess changing threats to the atmosphere
Target Area: Belize, Central America, Jungle
Keywords: Excessive rainfall. Smoke. Air pollution. Slash and burn agriculture. Warming. Environmental impact. Coastal flooding. Crops. Air quality. Respiratory illness. Disease. Species impact.

FIRE: Orleans
Rocky Mountain Region, Colorado, USA

Project Overview: *Wildfire in the West*
Constraints: Assess changing threats to forests
Target Area: Boulder & Steamboat Springs, Colorado, USA
Keywords: Drought. Water rights. Urban wildland interface. Fire suppression. Type 1 IHC interagency hotshots. Handcrew. Firefighting tradition. Species extinction. Crop impact. Ski industry. Humidity. Wind. Fire code. Disaster planning. Interagency cooperation.

WATER: Maps
Palau, Micronesia, South Pacific

Project Overview: *Warming Waters: Ocean Health*
Constraints: Assess the changing threat to oceans
Target Area: Palau, Micronesia. Access via live-aboard dive boat
Keywords: Ocean rise. Coral bleaching. Ocean acidification. Plastic pollution. Coastal Flooding. Illegal overfishing. Marine protected areas. Treaties. International Maritime Law. Coastal zones. Fish stocks. Navigational rights. Mineral claims. Coastal waters. Littoral zone.

DOESN'T' MAKE DOLLARS, DOESN'T MAKE SENSE

When she first joined GMISA, Bellony LaMarque instructed her staff to look into purchasing an abandoned industrial facility that lay dormant outside Skopje, Macedonia. When she pulled the trigger on that investment, she wasn't exactly sure what GMISA would use the dilapidated campus for, but at the time, it had been a great tax write-off and it offered possibilities. She had a pretty good idea that the demand for specialized pharmaceuticals would offer members a variety of new business opportunities, including growing markets for chemical precursors, diet supplements, and industrial chemicals. And she had been proven right.

Over the last few years, the business grew and the campus transformed. Today it was a modern chemical processing plant with specialized lines of business. When the opportunity arose to dabble in military contracts, it made business sense to expand further. LaMarque funded the construction of a biosafety level 4 (BSL-4) containment facility to accommodate the flood of money seeking bespoke development of new toxins, weaponized microbes, viruses, pathogens, and infectious materials. They needed a facility with equipment and technical skills to research antigenic shifts capable of delivering aerosolized variants of swine flu, avian flu, MERS, COVID, and Ebola to the highest bidders.

Biosafety engineering protocols were followed during the construction of the facility, although LaMarque kept tight control of costs. When it came to approving a budget for airlocks, positive-pressure doors, and filtering equipment for effluent decontamination, LaMarque cut corners. She considered her trade-offs reasonable, and proudly touted GMISA's commitment to safety to local officials whose approvals she needed. Those approvals were often obtained over lavish dinners featuring jovial toasts and endless shots of potent local rakija, a fruit brandy, along with barrels of popular Skopsko pilsner.

Secondhand industrial equipment and machinery left over from defunct Soviet military and space programs appeared well-suited to meet biocontainment requirements, and they were a bargain to boot. LaMarque provided an interview to a local magazine where she explained: *"GMISA is creating new jobs here. Our corporate commitment to safety and diversity is second to none!"* The interview concluded with one of her classic, colorful quotes: *"If it doesn't make dollars, it doesn't make sense!"*

LaMarque accepted several civic awards for outstanding corporate citizenship while she was schmoozing local officials and making rounds of the city. All was well for a time. Eastern European scientists with technical knowledge and skills were hungry for jobs and drawn to work at the lab. The team worked hard and succeeded in developing new variants of COVID-19 viruses, hemorrhagic fevers, and causative agents in the pursuit of scientific breakthroughs.

By 2027, the lab had an international reputation and a large, technically trained staff. The researchers were curious to learn what might be possible employing clustered regularly interspaced short palindromic repeats, or CRISPR, gene editing tools and techniques, along with other biotech. There had never been a major lab accident, and the safety team was proud of their ability to manage the dangerous work within acceptable safety margins.

With such a strong safety record and strict biohazard protocols in place, it was surprising that over a period of weeks that summer, no one noticed a slowly growing pile of powdery black rubber accumulating in a doorway in a remote corner of the complex.

That was the first sign of deteriorating neoprene rubber seals in one of the refurbished airlocks.

AIR

Kate Tong startled awake as her aircraft touched down at Philip S. W. Goldson International Airport in Belize City (BZE). She had a plan that would enable her to quickly surveil the impacts of air pollution and climate in this beautiful small country famous for rainforests, reefs, beaches, and its commitment to ecotourism.

She took a local bus from Belize City heading four hours northwest into the jungle of Cayo District. She planned on establishing her base of operations at Chaa Creek, a jungle lodge in San Ignacio close to the Guatemalan border. From Chaa Creek, she would work her way back to the coast, ending up on the tiny island of Caye Caulker. In these two different microclimates, she could effectively gather a variety of data and observe climate impacts up close.

Tong wasted no time. The challenges facing the small nation became obvious to her before she even got off the bus. The smell of burning, smoking, wet plant material was overpowering; then she saw flickering flames. The bus took her past jungle areas being cleared by the centuries-old technique called slash-and-burn. Wide swaths of forest were burned to make room for agriculture before her eyes. The extent of the burn was enormous, and she almost couldn't believe that what she was seeing was a deliberate initiative undertaken by local ranchers instead of an uncontrolled natural disaster.

Through thick and choking smoke, Tong could make out forms of men clad in rubber boots, wearing bandanas across their mouths as filters, swinging machetes to clear debris and encourage the burn. It was a chilling sight, one that impressed itself upon her deeply and set the tone for her stay. The bus drove on, but Tong's perspective had already shifted.

Before arriving, she'd done quite a bit of reading. It had not been hard to find details of the impact of climate change ravaging Belize after just a few minutes of searching online. The World Health Organization stated the air quality to be "moderately unsafe." Some of the contributors included the local petroleum industry, slash-and-burn agriculture, and vehicle emissions.

Sea level and temperature changes negatively impacted agricultural and fishing ecosystems, which in turn was affecting the livelihood of Belizeans, especially those who were disadvantaged. Due to greenhouse gases, destructive storms were becoming more regular—there were thirty named storms in 2020—which severely impacted the economic stability of the country.

Armed with a host of data, articles, studies, and reviews upon arriving at Chaa Creek, Tong got settled in her jungle bungalow and began planning her approach to gather more material and consider the impact of what she might find here. She toured the resort, grabbed a sorrel flower iced tea, changed into a swimsuit, and headed to the Macal River for a dip.

Tong floated awhile in the cool water, quieting her mind. She spent ten minutes focusing on the sounds, smells, and light of the jungle, listening intently to the river, bird calls, and insects. This was a technique a former Special Air Service (SAS) instructor had shared with her, a practice to accelerate familiarity and quickly become present and aware, to tune into the surroundings when first arriving in a new area of operations.

Feeling refreshed, Tong changed and headed to the main lodge for dinner. The menu included carrot and ginger soup flavored with orange peel and lemongrass. She chose cho cho cantaloupe salad with mango balsamic dressing, followed by fish wrapped in Santa Maria leaves and sprinkled with lime butter.

After talking with several guests during her meal, she made a plan for the following day. Tong would walk the Belize Medicinal Plants Trail to examine the health of the horticulture and learn about heirloom plants crucial to traditional Maya medicine. Then she would travel on horseback through the rainforest. She decided to also have a guide walk her through nearby Vaca Falls for a broader view of changes impacting the area.

Early the next morning, Tong waited for her hiking guide to arrive, wiping sweat from her face with a towel. It was already 102 degrees, 88 percent humidity. Soon, a battered and dust-spattered Land Rover Defender came to a stop in front of her. Out leaped a smiling guide, Candelaria Teresita, who vigorously shook her hand.

"You can call me Cande," she said.

Tong took in the young and wiry guide's knee-high rubber boots, long pants, and heavy, long-sleeve overshirt for hiking in this sticky, oppressive heat. She knew one thing right away. Cande was going to hike her into the ground.

The tiny Belizean oozed energy, confidence, and enthusiasm. A former rubber tapper, Teresita had grown up on a subsistence farm in Cayo, living in an open-air structure alongside her siblings, dogs, a giant anteater, and the occasional jaguar. Her family's life was organized around farming and gathering the papaya, cabbage, plantains, soursop, cacao, coconuts, and tomatoes flourishing in the area. For several years the British Army Training and Support Unit (BATSUB) outside Belize City had employed

Cande as a survival and navigation instructor supporting the garrison's jungle warfare training.

As they walked and got to know each other, Cande tried to impress upon Tong the key role Indigenous women were playing as the battle for the future of Earth's climate continued to unfold. Pointing to various items of interest along the path she explained: "Few tourists seem interested in learning more about our ancient wisdom and proven, sustainable ways." She paused.

Tong was paying attention.

"Mayans lived in harmony with the natural world for thousands of years. European settlers in centuries past viewed nature as an endless, unexplored wilderness, something apart from human life. The land was considered a savage force, something to be conquered. Indigenous populations of North and South America held the opposite view."

Cande and Tong chatted for hours on this topic as they hiked through dark shadows beneath the thick canopy, sweating with each humid step. Tong's clothes stuck to her skin, but she didn't mind. She was absorbed in her work, observing and recording everything while gathering the facts, stories, and natural history Cande was sharing.

Tong stopped to catalog an unusual flower. She used PlantNet, an app on her phone to photograph and identify interesting species of native plants as well as invasive specimens. Over years of study and on previous South American trips, Tong's "Plants of Central America" database had grown to nearly 5,600 species. Just in the two days she'd been onsite, she'd already added sixty-four species. Cande did not require an app, she was a walking encyclopedia of flora, fauna, and natural history and worked faster than any app Tong might open.

Cande stepped off the trail. She motioned to Tong, pointing at a large tree ensnared in vines. "Thirsty?"

"Sure," Tong replied. "Why are you pointing to a vine?"

"Water in the jungle," Cande began, "is critical to survival, yes?"

Tong agreed.

"See this? Water vine—pure, clean water. You will enjoy this."

With a smooth, practiced motion, Cande unsheathed her battered machete and struck the vine in the middle with blinding speed. The blow separated an end, which she offered Tong. Tong raised the cut vine to her mouth and drank, finding the water pure and refreshing. There was a lot of it in there. She used the last handful to wet her face and wipe away sweat and grime.

"Thank you; that is beautiful. Quite a lovely surprise. Are there any cold mojito vines hanging around here?"

Cande didn't get the joke.

Tong returned to data collection.

Farther down the trail, Cande stopped Tong in her tracks, urging her to remain perfectly still. They waited at a safe distance as a six-foot brown and gray fer-de-lance pit viper slithered across the trail. Known by locals as *tres minutos*, or "three minutes"—because that's how long you had to live if bitten—the highly venomous snakes were one of a half-dozen species of viper common across Belize. This one had been large enough to strike above the knee. Fortunately, if left alone, they usually chose to avoid human contact. The pair continued on.

As Tong heard interesting bird calls, she would call a stop and motion for silence so she could hold up her phone and allow its microphone to capture birdsongs in her Merlin Bird ID app. The app allowed Tong to rapidly capture, identify, and classify dozens of birds inhabiting a small area all at once, thus compiling a detailed list as she went.

Using the apps, her phone camera, and a few tools of her own, Tong's data collection was rapid and accurate, enabling her to capture, classify, and store in minutes hundreds of times the amount of environmental data that would have been possible even by a much larger team of researchers a few years ago.

The pair continued hiking. Tong peppered Cande with questions about her life growing up in Cayo. "What would your ancestors have done differently today, in terms of caring for the environment?"

"My ancestors had deep knowledge about managing their lands," Cande replied. "Growing and distributing food, understanding what constituted sustainable practices that nurtured the Earth so it would always provide for them—they lived *with* the land. To survive, they had to be resilient; they didn't have a choice. Their approach was based on reverence for the natural world, they had a passion for connecting to this land. They believed their lives were tied to it, that the land was itself a *living* force, a conscious being that provided life. They were good stewards of the land for this reason."

Tong echoed back what she'd just heard: "The land was part of a connected whole in which humans were just one more small part?"

"Yes. Today, those lessons of respect and stewardship could help educate anyone who chooses to learn. Sustainable agriculture, fisheries management, forests. Continuing traditional ways alongside new technology. We are experimenting here today with off-grid solar panels and regenerative solutions. We've always adapted, that's part of our approach.

Now we have to adapt faster, is all. It all comes down to this, Miss Kate. Environmental health and human health, they are the same."

Tong knew that in Belize, like most places where people were economically dependent upon natural resources, pressure to make money and meet growing commercial demand often led to over-hunting, over-fishing, soil exhaustion, and habitat loss, all of which eroded biological diversity.

And so, here we are, thought Tong. *Trying to shine a light on an existential threat.* "Cande, how have you managed to survive out here your whole life?" Tong wondered.

"How did I learn to survive in the jungle? To find food, build shelter, tap rubber trees, care for animals, train soldiers, and run a guide business for wealthy tourists?" She paused. "It's a flow—everything is a flow. Once you know the flow, you can do anything."

The pair sat down among rocks at Vaca Falls for lunch. Tong pulled out her battered leather Traveler's Notebook (TN) and K Series fountain pen, which she'd filled with turquoise Montblanc ink. She began jotting down observations, data, and ideas. The TN notebook was a Japanese system combining various paper inserts, connecting bands, pockets, and stickers. Tong was a pretty good sketch artist; she began filling pages with sketches of the water vine, flowers, an anteater, a snake, and a cameo of Cande.

After their long day of hiking was over, Tong returned to her Chaa Creek bungalow. The door was ajar, and her belongings were strewn about, bedding on the floor, and drawers left open. Someone had been in here, looking for . . . what? It appeared nothing was missing, and no one was there now. She got busy straightening up.

Whoever it was had tipped their hand. Should she report this to the hotel management? No, better to continue observing and collecting data until she knew who she was up against. She suspected this was a warning, or an attempt to steal her field research, but she also couldn't help but remember the car that had so recently tried to shove Orleans off a cliff.

Was someone monitoring the work of the Maps Private Value team? Tong wanted to send off a summary, upload some data, and provide a warning to Rave and Mait via MPV's secure cloud wiki. She pulled out her phone, opened the template and dictated a note before happy hour began.

TOP SECRET / HCS-P / SI-G / TK / FGI / RSEN / ORCON / NOFORN / FISA

RE: UNIPCC CONTRACT CONTROL NUMBER #S-2654 GLOBAL CLIMATE CHANGE: BELIZE

Successful onsite data collection. Ecological stability deteriorating. Loss of arable farmland, slash and burn agriculture. Rising water and strengthening storms impact coastal infrastructure.

Room searched, nothing of value lost. Will relocate immediately offshore to Caye Caulker and check health of Belize Barrier Reef from there.

End

In addition to everything she'd learned here in the jungle, Tong discovered the Chaa Creek bar crafted a delicious mojito with a ton of freshly picked mint leaves from the garden in back. *You can't get this from a vine*, she thought while sipping delightedly.

The next morning, she met Cande for a breakfast consisting of egg quesadillas, coffee, fruit, freshly squeezed juices, and dessert bowls filled with rich, creamy orange bavarois covered with orange salsa, Cande offered to join Tong for the short flight from San Ignacio to Caye Caulker.

"I have a friend who owns a café on the island and serves the best conch salad. Mind if I tag along? I'm PADI certified."

PADI, the Professional Association of Diving Instructors, certified divers and operated dive centers around the world.

Tong figured it made sense to have Cande join; she'd been good company in the jungle. Her knowledge of flora and fauna had proven encyclopedic, and it would be good to have a dive buddy Tong was familiar with once they reached the reef. "Sure, love to have you along," Tong replied, spooning a thick mouthful of bavarois.

As she finished her coffee, Tong opened the NetJets app on her phone. She logged in using the Maps Private Value account and paid for a private air charter with flight credits Rave provided, securing the only aircraft available in the area, a brand-new Pilatus PC-12 NGX.

The versatile ten-passenger, Swiss-made turboprop was popular with charter operators, special mission agencies, and law enforcement for its reliability, options, and use of low-emission sustainable aviation fuel. The short takeoff or landing (STOL) special mission aircraft might be overkill for a forty-minute hop to Caye Caulker, but in Tong's defense, it was all that was available on short notice, and there was a logistics question concerning the nearby San Ignacio town airstrip. A STOL aircraft would be well-suited for operating in and out of the remote, unpaved airfield here, as well as landing on the small island.

Just before logging off, Tong noticed the NetJets app included a "catering preferences" button. She clicked it, examining her options. Tong knew from experience that pressurization inside aircraft cabins dulled sweet and salty flavors.

"Cande, you okay with buffalo chicken dip and miso-glazed salmon inflight?" Tong teased. She already knew the two dishes would hold up flavor-wise at altitude. and would pair perfectly with the champagne cocktails she added for the brief ride. Besides, it was exactly what Rave Maps would have done.

With those details out of the way, Tong opened up TripAdvisor and booked two rooms at an island cabana on Caye Caulker, along with a dive tour that would get them out for a look at the Belize Barrier Reef. They could begin collecting data on one small section of the 190-mile-long underwater ecosystem.

Tong called the Chaa Creek front desk, checked out, and ordered a Land Rover for the short ride over to San Ignacio's airstrip. Less than an hour later, Kate and Cande were the only two passengers there, seated beneath the only shade tree in the entire valley.

The pair watched as the Pilatus swooped in right on time, landing with a small puff of dust. It turned and taxied back toward them. With the engine still running, a hostess dropped the stairs and welcomed them aboard, helping with their bags and getting them seated. In a moment, they were belted in, and the powerful PT6 engine revved once more. The craft seemed to float up into the air with almost no effort. Born to fly.

It was so quiet in the cabin that Tong easily overheard the cork popping on a chilled bottle of Veuve Clicquot.

FIRE

Mait traveled to Denver to begin researching fire ecology. She wanted to learn how it impacted Rocky Mountain residents, forests, and wildlife as well as try to determine what had changed over the past decade. Before heading north to Steamboat Springs, she decided to tour the scene of the Marshall Fire, Colorado's most destructive wildfire, one that had devastated a thousand homes and businesses in Boulder County in December 2021, resulting in several billion dollars in insurance claims. Extraordinarily high winds had whipped several small fires into a raging inferno. She'd read the fire began in the grassy outskirts of a suburban area and spread at remarkable speed.

To jumpstart her research Mait texted Chance Cole, an old friend and wildland firefighter for the U.S. Forest Service.

CC had spent many hard seasons leading Type 1 Interagency Hotshots, legendary handcrews who worked wildland forest fires in the Rockies. CC helped work the Marshall Fire because his home had been in Superior, the neighborhood most affected. "Had been," was the correct tense; his house, like so many others, was long gone. He was happy to walk Mait around and explain what he'd seen that day.

The pair met over hot Polish sausage hot dogs slathered with relish, sauerkraut, and mustard at the Costco food court in Superior, fifteen minutes south of Boulder. CC had been in the store shopping for groceries and last-minute Christmas presents around noon on December 30, 2021, when the blaze began. He had just popped a sample of barbecued chicken in his mouth when he heard a sheriff's deputy run through the store screaming orders at shoppers. "Leave your stuff. Fire at the back of the store. Evacuate now. Head east! Leave your stuff. Head toward Denver. Evacuate now!"

It had been a beautiful and sunny winter morning when CC entered the store. When he made it outside with all the other shoppers who'd abandoned their carts inside, he couldn't believe the scene before him.

One hundred miles per hour winds whipped thick smoke and ash across the parking lot. Parents holding kids fought to open their car doors against the wind as smoke and toxic airborne debris swirled around them. Smoke was already so thick it blotted out the sun. Everything appeared in mottled, dystopian shades of gray and brown. He couldn't see far; maybe forty feet in front of him.

CC quickly made his way home and hustled to ensure his wife, kids, and dogs got out. His wife, Dakota, knew him well enough not to start arguing; she could see he was amped up. Besides, one look out the window was all it took for her to go to battle stations. She focused on getting the children to safety. She made sure they were packed and out the door amid a storm of shouting, tantrums, and tears. She had her three kids, as well as two neighborhood playmates who'd come over just an hour before. The chocolate chip cookies they'd baked were cooling on the counter.

She told CC to meet them at the Denver Airport Marriott when he could. This was part of the disaster communication plan they'd created years ago.

CC kept three Yeti box go-bags in the garage full of sleeping bags, food, blankets, and flashlights. He pushed the boxes in the back with the dogs as they got all the kids and their backpacks loaded up. He had the presence of mind to toss in a bag of the one thing pet owners always forgot when evacuating in an emergency: dog food.

Dakota jumped in front and began driving the battered, heavily loaded Ford Expedition. With both hands white knuckling the wheel, she picked her way through choking, thick smoke and high wind, swerving to avoid vehicles already abandoned haphazardly at crazy angles in her neighborhood streets while yelling into her phone for Siri to dial the parents of the other children. It was mayhem. Eventually, they made it to the highway and headed east where the air was clear. Nothing else mattered.

CC got busy helping the local sheriff go door to door in his neighborhood, encouraging everyone to get out. The first couple CC encountered, his neighbors down the street, were unwilling to get in gear and leave. Longtime residents, they appeared calm and thoughtful, insisting to the officers they'd be okay. They wanted to remain in their home.

At this point, everyone was coughing and wheezing from airborne soot, standing at the front door, yelling over the unrelenting howl of wind and crackling of nearby homes already engulfed in flames. CC had seen homeowners experience this combination of stubbornness, denial, and shock before. To save time, he had no choice but to be blunt. He began yelling over the wind.

"That's fine. We can't make you leave your home. It's okay. You can stay," he said, screaming to be heard, his throat raw. "Listen, these officers need to get going. Please—write down for me the name of your dentist."

The man looked puzzled. CC continued. "The police are gonna need your dental records when this is over. That'll help us with the identification."

After a moment, the couple ran inside to grab their dog and headed for their car. CC and the officers ran down the street, yelling at everyone to get out now. He ran door to door as he watched his neighborhood burn, along with the one next to it. The playground swings were melting in the park where he often took his kids.

A long family history of wildland firefighting kept CC committed to his dangerous firefighter seasonal job. He surely didn't stick around for the pay, which was $10 an hour with no benefits. He and his team would spend long months away from home working remote blazes, beating, or pounding out brush fires with basic garden tools like shovels and rakes as well as pulaskis (a combination axe and hoe used in forestry) before each blaze grew larger. Camaraderie and tradition were everything.

When they weren't working an incident, CC and his team spent hours at makeshift helibases in Idaho, Utah, or Colorado, killing time before they were called out again. Two weeks on, and two days off. The handcrews would find ways to while away downtime working out, sleeping, texting loved ones, cooking, or picking over meals-ready-to-eat. "Chili-Mac Macaroni and Beef in Sauce" and "Mexican-Style Chicken Stew Entrée" were popular MREs. Those two were highly prized, and frequent trading was a constant. The military rations could be eaten straight out of the pouch, and enjoyed a long, stable shelf life despite mostly being not that enjoyable.

CC tied a wet bandanna around his face to help filter the sooty, thick smoke, much denser and hotter now. For some reason at that moment, he recalled the bulletin board back at one of those nameless base gyms they'd staged out of, and amid the chaos, he began chuckling, trying not to inhale more smoke as he laughed. Some wiseass had pinned a flyer up taunting:

"You Can Do Incredible Things Here. Now Hiring Smiling Faces. $20/hour. McDonald's."

CC continued describing his recollection to Mait as the pair walked through neighborhood after neighborhood of scorched building foundations and bare soil that had once been neatly manicured, grassy yards and gardens. Six years after the fire, the mineral smell of burned soil still filled their nostrils, their boots kicking up puffs of ash.

"I heard the fire caused local water systems to lose power, making it harder to combat the flames," CC said. "Water distribution depressurization spread quickly, compounded by failure of backup power. The combination degraded what little firefighting support had been brought to bear early on."

Mait recognized the familiar sequence, the failure cascade she'd seen too many times. She turned to CC. "I assume once your evacuations were complete there was nothing left to do."

"Yes. Incident commanders notified utilities to turn off gas, water, and electricity from central," CC muttered. "Time had come; let the flames burn, burn till they were done. **Maybe we built too close to WUI.**"

"WUI?" asked Mait.

"Wildland-urban interface."

CC had fought enough wildfire to know tactics that worked. As he explained, Mait watched his face. She could see him reliving the moment with a pained expression.

"We normally try to use geography and wind to our advantage when we fight wildfires. We count on day-to-night temperature shifts to help us make progress. We control large fires by setting small ones, and use natural barriers, rocks, rivers, and cliffs to contain the blaze and get it under control."

He'd watched from the tops of canyons as huge tankers zoomed low, following rivers nap-of-the-earth, twisting and turning the aircraft between canyon walls and dropping retardant on hard-to-reach hotspots.

Out where most wildfires took place—in the wild—the Hotshots could cut trees and work on setting up fire lines. But not on that December day in Superior. CC tried to sum it up: "I've never seen anything burn with the ferocity and speed of this fire as it moved across this bone-dry grassland, driven by intense winds during a time of drought, burning homes over nine square miles.

"I saw wooden fences, decks, grasses, trees, and power lines serve as fire conduits spreading flame home to home, while flying embers carried destruction farther. After the fire had been extinguished, there were lingering health effects that began impacting residents coming from volatile compounds in melted homes, vehicles, and furniture. Benzene and hydrocarbons were released by the heat, while the metals dissolved in ash. Toxic."

Mait said nothing. She let her friend relive the moment and finish sharing his trauma.

After a long silence he said, "Mait, I came to realize at that moment how unprepared all of us were to deal with wildland fire of this size and intensity. I remember standing on this very hill, watching as flames engulfed my neighborhood, then my own home." His eyes teared as he relived the horror, and for the gratitude he felt today knowing his family had made it out.

This hadn't been a rural area in the middle of nowhere where he and his team were normally tasked. This had been home. Now it was gone. After expressing her empathy and profound thanks, Mait said her goodbyes and left CC. She summoned an electric Uber to shuttle her to busy Centennial Airport (APA), 15 miles south of Denver.

During the six years Mait spent living in Toronto, she had put in the time and earned her pilot's license at Billy Bishop Toronto City Airport (YTZ). Bishop had been a World War 1 Canadian flying ace; when the airport opened in 1939, this single strip on the island was Toronto's main aviation hub. Orleans loved learning to fly out of YTZ, the waters of Lake Ontario beckoning at either end of the runway. Turning onto final approach felt like landing on an aircraft carrier docked alongside the glistening Harbourfront.

As a licensed pilot, Orleans was qualified to fly herself for the next leg of her journey over the Continental Divide to Steamboat Springs. With the NetJets app and Rave's login, she secured an electric Beta Technologies CX300 for the 190-mile journey north to Bob Adams Airport (SBS) near downtown Steamboat. Mait was aware of unpredictable winds, weather, and icing conditions inherent in mountain flying. She was confident in her skills and the battery-powered aircraft itself, which featured a unique design, pusher prop, and range over 300 miles.

While the batteries charged, she grabbed lunch upstairs at the Perfect Landing, the storied Denver restaurant and aviator hangout. The walls here were lined with flight memorabilia, paintings of fighter aircraft, and astronaut mementos. Floor-to-ceiling glass windows afford a view of the runway and busy ramp area bustling with private jets, helicopters, and military hardware.

The lunch crowd today was an eclectic mix of pilots, travelers, and a few Jeppesen navigation staff whose offices sat over on the other side of the runway. Mait chose a Mile High Club sandwich with fries and an Arnold Palmer iced tea and lemonade. When she was finished, she paid her bill and walked downstairs to the front desk at jetCenter, the FBO, or fixed base operator. This was where private pilots checked weather, filed flight plans, recharged and fueled aircraft, and coordinated ground services.

Once she taxied out and got airborne, Orleans headed northwest over Denver. The view from the cockpit was incredible. There wasn't a cloud in the sky, though Mait did notice haze hugging the horizon. Woodsmoke, probably from faraway wildfires in New Mexico. It was perfect flying weather.

She followed Highway 70 west, turned north over Empire, and made her way up and over Berthoud Pass to Winter Park. She could see thousands of acres of standing dead lodgepole pine. Enormous swaths of forest had been ravaged by beetle kill that began in 2009, a result of drought and warming temperatures that encouraged pine beetles and fungus to spread across thousands of square miles of the stately pines, killing them all.

She flew low over the Yampa Valley and buzzed downtown Steamboat lining up for runway 32. Mait stated her intention over the open frequency for the uncontrolled airport, zipped across the threshold at 80 knots, and stuck the landing. As Mait taxied up to the terminal and parked at a tie-down, her exotic aircraft drew a crowd of enthusiastic onlookers. She made the most of the moment, stepping down from the cabin unzipping her USN G1 goatskin flight jacket and flipping up her mouton fur collar, striking a pose for Insta while shaking her long hair, sporting a big smile. She was reminded of 1930s snapshots she'd seen showing pilot Amelia Earhart posing and smiling impishly beside her silver Lockheed Electra before she was lost mysteriously in the Pacific.

The dryness in the air was palpable here in Steamboat; Mait could feel it pulling moisture from her skin. She knew at this 7,000-foot altitude she needed to remain hydrated.

As she checked into Steamboat FBO to find transportation into town, she inquired about the two black airport cats who used to rule the roost in the passenger terminal when there was daily commercial service here. Mait was sorry to learn they had passed away long ago. She'd once observed the pair in action during a ski trip, they had been strutting around calming passengers nervous about mountain flying on the "vomit comet"—the legendary seventy-seat de Havilland Canada DHC-7 bush plane that used to make a daily hop over the Divide to Denver.

As Orleans grabbed her flight bag and stepped outside, she registered the smell of acrid wildfire smoke, noticeable now the wind had changed. Hiking and biking would be out of the question. Normal air quality in Steamboat stood around Air Quality Index, or AQI, 30. The current AQI was 140, and there were warnings to remain indoors.

It was getting late in the afternoon, so Orleans headed over to the ski area for a sunset ride up Steamboat Silver Bullet gondola. From the deck on top of Thunderhead Lodge, she would have a commanding view of the area to the west. The volume of particulate matter in the air made for a dramatic red and gold sunset, although the beautiful sight was tinged with sadness as she knew what made it so breathtaking. Wildfire weather conditions were becoming more frequent and intense, lasting longer than in the past. The combination of high heat, low humidity, and strong wind created dangerous conditions. The southern part of Colorado was seeing one additional month of wildfire weather per year now, compared with fifty years ago.

Orleans placed her daypack on the ground, leaning against the gondola building. She began shooting photos and capturing video with her Ray-Ban Meta Smart Glasses while narrating temperature, humidity, elevation, direction, and geospatial data into her soundtrack.

When she was finished, she turned to see her backpack no longer sat where she had placed it. Orleans took a quick look around then ran to the railing of the observation deck. She saw a hooded figure on a mountain bike wearing her pack pedaling full speed, racing down Flying Diamond, a singletrack bike path. She snapped a pic with the glasses, but there was no way she was going to catch the thief.

Fortunately, there had been little of value in the bag, only a water bottle and sweatshirt. *Hell's bells*, Orleans thought to herself. Tong had just warned her to keep a weather eye open for trouble.

To be sure her data made it to the team safely, Orleans fired off a quick update to the secure cloud wiki as the gondola made its way down the hill.

TOP SECRET / HCS-P / SI-G / TK / FGI / RSEN / ORCON / NOFORN / FISA

RE: UNIPCC CONTRACT CONTROL NUMBER #S-2654
GLOBAL CLIMATE CHANGE: UNITED STATES / COLORADO

Wildfire damage. Poor air quality. Drought. Airborne particulate matter from smoke. Damage to communities in wildland-urban interface.

Bag stolen. Maintaining situational awareness. Continuing to collect data.
End

Mait left the ski area and headed downtown to get her evening started. She thought she'd kill two birds with one stone at the independent Steamboat bookstore and café, Off the Beaten Path, where she could search local information about history and weather in the area over a cocktail. Mait was curious to see if local lore might provide a historical perspective on how weather impacted the economic history of the valley. She picked up a stack of local books, grabbed a table and a glass of white Burgundy, then sat down and learned that for thousands of years, elk and bison in the Yampa Valley had been food for Indigenous people.

As she read on, the café filled. A stranger asked if he could share her table. "Sure," Mait replied. Once he sat down, she asked the man what he did. He was a volunteer at the nearby Tread of Pioneers Museum.

Mait asked what he knew of the economic history of the Yampa Valley. He launched into a detailed historical description as he sipped a caramel cinnamon latte. "Nomadic Ute tribes were followed by trappers here in the 1820s drawn by the promise of beaver pelts. Trapping gave way to panning for gold, then mining, then grazing cattle took off, making use of the wet, fertile valley floors.

"After the introduction of the railroad in 1910, coal mining became the largest business. The railroad provided the means to move large quantities of coal to market and brought more settlers to the area. Skiing and tourism took their place as economic drivers beginning in the 1960s."

Mait quizzed the man further. "Would you say climate-driven weather had always been an important element in strategies for survival here?"

"Yes. There's no question that is true," he replied. "Back then, it was the Ute spending summers hunting in the mountains, then moving to lower elevation during cold winters. Today, ski area managers make decisions about how much water to commit to making snow. Vacationers hope to time vacation trips and catch some legendary Champagne Powder.

"People have always had to think a bit before they commit resources, money, and time, making decisions whether it's about hunting, when to plant, when to harvest, or what to invest in and when. Those decisions affect their futures, their livelihoods, as well as the income and security of thousands of staff and families."

"What everyone wants to know is, what will happen next?" Mait asked. "How long will the growing season be? Are we looking at a drought? Fire? Flood? Extreme heat? An early freeze? A blizzard?

"Here," said the man, standing up and grabbing a book off a shelf by their table. He handed it to Mait. She turned over the cover; it was a copy of *The Old Farmer's Almanac.*

"You're asking about the weather. This used to be the bible for answering the questions you are asking. Some think it still is. This describes full moon dates, planting dates, and folklore. It also makes weather predictions and shares weather data. Climate is different though. Long-term patterns that emerge from weather data over, say, thirty years? That is climate."

Mait thanked the man as he slipped on his Norwegian Wool cashmere down car coat. He insisted on paying both his bill and hers, then generously tipped the bookstore staff.

Mait flipped pages of the *Almanac*, stopping to scan a chapter entitled "Home Remedies: Cures, Charms, Ointments, and Prescribed Undertakings."

When she peered back up, the man was gone.

WATER

Rave was watching a dramatic sunset reflecting off the western Pacific while she comfortably stretched out on a deck chair. She was warming herself on the aft deck of *Palau Ironwood*, a forty-meter luxury liveaboard motor sailing and dive boat. She was catching the last rays of the sun in preparation for tonight's night dive. Captain Bluch Ralm was a longtime skipper familiar with Micronesian tides, hazards, and local waters of Palau's Rock Islands; he had come highly recommended.

Rave heard the captain issue orders to his crew as they set up oxygen tanks, lights, and buoyancy compensators. Ralm had chosen this spot so his liveaboard guests could observe the biggest nightly vertical migration of marine creatures on Earth. Millions of tons of marine biomass rose each evening from the dark depths of the mesopelagic layer, moving toward the dim illumination of the epipelagic layer close to the surface where they would feed and mate. Ralm described the nightly process as the "diel vertical migration": "Jellies, gastropods, cephalopods, and hundreds of species of fish and larvae make this journey each evening. You will not be disappointed!"

Rave glanced at her shipmates. She'd gotten to know them in the week they'd been aboard. Each diver was absorbed in donning and adjusting wetsuits, masks, fins, tanks, and weight belts. There was the young Canadian couple on their honeymoon, Doug and Cathy Livingston from Victoria, British Columbia. Alex and Olivia Battersea were a retired couple from Houston who had owned a successful real estate business. The Volle family of San Diego rounded out the guest roster; Martin, Naomi, and the college-age twins, Kai, and her brother, Namiko.

Everyone had various levels of experience diving in storied resorts around the world. Palau stood at the top of the bucket list for all of them due to its natural beauty, diverse marine life, caverns, drop-offs, and shipwrecks.

Earlier in the day the twins had been playful and outspoken as the group enjoyed a unique local experience snorkeling nearby Jellyfish Lake, where five million golden jellyfish evolved to lose their sting. Swimming among them as they migrated across the lake daily was a dream. The twins were quiet and subdued now. Perhaps they were a bit apprehensive contemplating their first open ocean night dive.

Once all was ready, one by one, each of the divers switched on their flashlight and dive computer and entered the water. Rave rolled in backward off the gunwale, keeping one hand over her mask and regulator to hold them in place.

She followed the guide down, focusing her gaze along the beam of her flashlight, which illuminated an astounding array of tiny creatures drifting past. Rave focused on slowing her breathing, maintaining a steady cadence. She thought of diving as a moving meditation. She enjoyed consciously slowing her oxygen consumption so she could remain submerged as long as possible. Rave felt her heart rate slow; she let her thoughts and cares slip away. She calmed her mind, opened her awareness, and centered herself.

Rave felt at home in the water, and she continued descending, breathing slowly and evenly, occasionally pinching her nose and blowing into it, a technique known as the Valsalva maneuver, to clear pressure in her ears. Opening herself to the melody of sea sounds and the mass of marine life around her, Rave began reflecting on what she'd learned about Micronesia from her research and what she'd observed this week.

Warming ocean temperatures had already caused a massive coral bleaching event in Palau in 1998. The effect of that remained pervasive, as Rave observed on several of her dives from *Palau Ironwood.* Looking over long stretches of dead white coral standing utterly barren, quiet, and devoid of marine life struck Rave powerfully; it was like a blow to the gut to get a close look at the slow-motion disaster.

Corals were living animals; they relied upon symbiont bacteria and cellular creatures that sheltered within them to sustain them. This relationship provided oxygen, nutrition, and energy for the coral to grow. When excessive heat or marine environmental pollutant chemicals killed the symbionts, coral tissue died and turned white. It looked bleached and could no longer serve as a shelter for fish and marine life.

Ralm and his crew knew a lot about the topic; they happily shared their thoughts after each dive, chatting over sliced fresh fruit and a few cold Red Roosters, a specialty local wheat beer from Palau Brewing.

Rave observed that pockets of coral communities around the Palauan archipelago were thriving. Though the Rock Islands had recently experienced consistently higher water temperature and heatwaves, some coral continued to appear normal and healthy on cooler outer reefs. That indicated one species of thermally tolerant coral was evolving with the threat, offering hope for the future.

Typhoons and storm surges were growing in strength driven by warming water temperatures. At the same time, drought driven by El Niño winds was becoming a challenge on land. Rave had read that in 2016, drought was so severe the Koror reservoir dried up entirely, and the city's main river dropped 80 percent, resulting in crop failure and food shortages.

Rave suspected the next likely impact of these converging trends would be rising sea levels. Saltwater inundation had already begun threatening coastal freshwater sources. Other low-lying infrastructure like schools, transportation, and cultural sites along the water's edge were at risk. The data she'd collected pointed to a connection between the changing climate and the destruction of natural habitats driven by growth and settlement.

Not to mention a new, alarming connection to pandemics.

As habitat evolved with the expansion of community housing and roads, the mix of plants, insects, and animals changed with it. Human-animal contact became more prevalent, driven by closer proximity to bats, monkeys, birds, pigs, and other animals. She heard from Mait that increased cross-species contact was prevalent in too-close Colorado urban-wildland interfaces; moose, elk, and bear frequented downtown streets of tony ski resorts. Coyotes and mountain lions took domestic pets from sidewalks and backyards more and more frequently.

Wherever it took place, increased cross-species interaction meant outbreaks of zoonotic diseases. The thought haunted her as she watched thick clouds of zooplankton, phytoplankton, jellyfish, squid, and sharks pass through the tunnel beam of her flashlight. Feeding, hunting, and mating were all part of the rich nightly migration toward the surface. Outside her small cone of light, all was darkness.

Having spent forty-five minutes underwater, it was time to begin heading back to the surface. The guide signaled the group to begin heading up. The eight divers made a five-minute safety stop fifteen feet beneath the surface, a procedure designed to help prevent decompression sickness.

They slowly ascended back to the surface and removed their masks. While bobbing gently in the swells, Rave was struck by the quiet and the beauty of a clear night sky full of bright stars. Beautiful. Then another thought struck her.

Where is the dive boat?

Their calls and shining flashlights did not elicit a response. They saw no lights and heard no engine. After several minutes of searching, the severity of the situation struck home. They were adrift in the Pacific Ocean at night. Alone.

And far from shore.

Rave knew currents in this area would draw them west if they didn't act. All that was out there for a thousand miles was open ocean.

Next stop, the Philippines.

Seeing their guide was perplexed and at a loss, Rave took charge. Before they'd rolled backward into the water, she'd checked her wrist compass and taken a bearing on the next island to the south, Peleliu. If they stuck together—and were very lucky—they might drift closer to the small island, which was infamous for horrific fighting that took place there in World War II. This was the only possible move.

Rave employed her command voice, the one she used to use as an Air Force officer. "Listen, everyone. This is a serious situation, but we can make a plan. Peleliu is to our south, that way. The current is going to carry us west. If we take our time and swim together through the evening, we will make it to shore by morning. I don't see any other choice here. Does everyone agree?"

There was startled murmuring and Rave could sense rising panic. Someone began a bit of panicked chatter, almost talking to themselves out loud. Not good. Rave could hear several stifled sobs. One of the twins? She couldn't tell in the dark. Their Palauan dive guide agreed and focused on Rave to make the call; he could sense her natural authority.

Rave knew focused activity would provide a diversion and help calm the group. She didn't want to oversell that everything was fine; it most definitely was not. But she knew from long experience if there was ever a time to make a plan, work it, and hope for the best, this was it.

Plan, Work, and Hope, that was the winning prescription for those who had survived unimaginably challenging disaster scenarios. Like this one. "Drop your weight belts and tanks, everyone. Do it now," commanded Rave.

After a moment's confusion and hesitation, the tourists began fumbling with buckles and clips. Soon all the heavy gear dropped away.

"Okay. I want you to relax for a moment. Inflate your BC, and your SMB too so I can see you. We're going to stay together, and we're all going to be okay." Anxious divers blew into tubes to fill their buoyancy compensator vests and then their surface marker buoys, which resembled large, vertically oriented, orange sausages, adding visibility to divers in the water. Soon eight safety sausages stood at attention, swaying in unison with the swell. Rave checked that everyone's vest was inflated and encouraged them to keep their masks dangling around their necks, to relax, and to begin swimming slowly to conserve energy. Her hope was to slow the dehydration that would be their greatest threat soon. Besides being lost in the ocean, of course.

They'd started the dive just after sunset, so it was full dark at this point. They swam through the calm of the evening, keeping close together. Rave heard a sob and dropped back to offer encouragement. She checked her compass frequently to ensure they were headed in the right direction, hoping the current was not carrying them too far west, and that sharks inhabiting these waters wouldn't find them of interest tonight. At one point the twins began singing a popular song, but they soon faded, their voices silenced by dehydration and despair.

During a rest stop, the group formed a circle, held hands, and checked in with each other. At this point, they'd been in the water nine hours, though it seemed longer. Cathy who was a teacher, told a story explaining that courage always lives within inside. She'd learned it from an elderly Israeli woman who'd lost her husband and both sons in several long-ago Mideast regional conflicts: "When crisis strikes and you need to find courage, that's the moment you find it's been inside you all along," she had shared.

A moment later Cathy herself teared up and stifled a sob. Several others muttered quiet prayers. Lethargy and acceptance were setting in. Rave noted these signs as she monitored the group while teetering on exhaustion herself. She continued to offer encouragement where it was needed.

At 4:00 AM, with people struggling to remain awake, and after talking had ceased, Rave caught a glimmer of light reflecting off a cloud on the horizon, an indication they were nearing Klouklubed, the single town on Peleliu. It was all she needed. "Look everyone; see that light?" she croaked, still trying to sound positive through her deep exhaustion. "It's a reflection from town. C'mon. We're nearly there."

Filled with renewed hope, they began kicking their swim fins with purpose, driving toward shore. It took two more hours of effort and left everyone completely spent, but by 6:00 AM, they were crawling ashore up rubble-strewn Orange Beach, the very same spot where many US Marines had given their lives scrambling forward under Japanese fire in September 1944.

All that greeted the group of exhausted divers this morning was an empty beach littered with coral rubble and the green jungle beyond. It was very quiet. After a brief rest and some relieved groans and tears from the group, Rave stripped off her wetsuit and gear. She addressed the group, all of whom lay prone across the sand too exhausted to move. 'Stay here and rest, everyone. I'm heading to town to find transportation. We made it!"

Wearing her swimsuit and neoprene dive booties that squished with each squeaky step, Rave staggered forward and found a footpath leading from the beach to the Southern Access, the single road to town. She was careful to stay on the road. Several million bombs had been dropped across the small island in 1944 as part of the fighting and not all of them had exploded. Yet.

Rave turned north, following the road to town, placing one foot in front of the other, walking in a bit of a daze, dehydrated and beginning to overheat as the sun rose. She was alive. She remained analytical enough to note that the white, packed coral road still bore the imprint of tank treads from over eighty years ago.

The following evening, Rave lay on the bed in her room in Koror thinking over the past forty-eight hours. She'd stopped a local driver and returned to Orange Beach to pick up the group who had recovered somewhat. Everyone was safely returned to the marina, and after a hastily procured snack and lots of water, they took the ferry back over to Koror. A huge meal that was alternatively raucous and tearstained followed, all of them bonded by their trauma. All that was left then was to notify the authorities what had taken place. The police took a report and promised to look into the matter, but so far there had been no indications of a missing vessel, and no sign of Ralm and his crew.

Each of the passengers took Rave aside to thank her personally, recognizing her leadership, and acknowledging it had been her determination that had seen them through. They thanked her profusely, exchanging numbers and promises to stay in touch. The twins insisted on snapping selfies with Rave and had already posted excitedly about the harrowing adventure and their new friend, the heroic value engineer Rave Maps.

Before allowing herself to drift off to sleep, Rave thought about the missing dive boat. It had to have been a deliberate attempt on their lives. *More specifically*, she thought, *on my life.* Who would do such a thing?

Rave dictated an update to MPV's secure cloud wiki before drifting off to sleep.

TOP SECRET / HCS-P / SI-G / TK / FGI / RSEN / ORCON / NOFORN / FISA

RE: UNIPCC CONTRACT CONTROL NUMBER #S-2654 GLOBAL CLIMATE CHANGE: PALAU

Ecological impact on agriculture, fishing, reefs. Research disrupted, dive boat missing, tourist group stranded at sea. No lives lost.

Maintain situational awareness and continue collecting data.

End

END OF THE RAINBOW

Lady Elliot Island was an Australian bird sanctuary and eco-resort on the Great Barrier Reef, fifty miles off the coast of Bundaberg, Queensland. It was the southernmost island on the reef, dedicated to educating guests on ways to protect marine life while reducing energy, waste, and water, and teaching them to take action once they returned home.

With her data collection effort in Palau wrapped up, Rave flew from Koror to Sydney. She took a bus north to Brisbane and made a brief stop at the University of Queensland (UQ) library seeking to learn more about the history of the bushfire crisis here on the mainland. Then she would hop aboard the small bush plane in Bundaberg that ferried guests the fifty miles offshore to the island.

Wildland fire information collected over the past five years by a team of university researchers has been cataloged into an online archive. As she reviewed the material, Rave could see the researchers had tracked the impact of burns driven by continually rising temperatures and severe drought across an enormous area of southeast Australia. Much of the devastation had taken place south of Sydney, in Victoria and New South Wales. Thousands of homes were destroyed by fast-moving bushfires in 2020, which also killed tens of thousands of sheep and farm animals, kangaroos, koalas, and other species.

The Australian Government Bureau of Meteorology has determined the country warmed more than a degree over the past century. Fires were starting earlier in the season, taking more of a toll on old eucalyptus forests and dried swamps formerly considered less likely to burn. More alarming now was an overlap between Northern and Southern Hemisphere fire seasons.

The first impact had been seen in struggles to share firefighting air tankers, something that would prove to be less manageable when more fires began burning at the same time. Understanding fire protection planning and management was now a rising priority among Australian policymakers who had previously struggled to acknowledge the implications of what constituents were experiencing. Rave finished doom-scrolling the database, got back on another bus, and closed her eyes until she arrived at Bundaberg (BDB) airport.

Rave soon touched down on Lady Elliot. As she stepped onto the crushed coral runway her ears filled with *kit, kit, kit*—the cries of a hundred thousand black noddy *Anous minutus* tropical seabirds who made the island their home. After checking in and unpacking in her hut, an outfitter tent with a wood frame and small deck in front, she threw on a swimsuit and headed to the water for a dip.

She came up short at the water's edge. A number of small black fins darted swiftly through water two feet from the shore. Epaulette sharks. It was a thrill to see them up close. She lay back on the sand, tuning into the sounds of the birds, wind, and waves. Perfect.

After a nap, Rave decided to get up and walk the beach around the island. Fifty feet wide, consisting of fine coral rubble, sand, and pebbles, it was easy walking. Circumnavigating the hundred-acre island took only forty-five minutes. Soon enough, Rave was looking at her own footprints in the sand.

Getting the afternoon started with rum punch and beer-battered flathead at the Beach Front Café seemed like a brilliant idea while she waited for the rest of the team to arrive.

Several hours later, Mait Orleans and Kate Tong stepped down onto the crushed coral runway, arriving to big hugs all around.

"Great to see you, Rave!" exclaimed Tong. She took one look around at the tiny atoll; the crushed coral airstrip extending from one side of the island to the other. "I love it here already!"

"We're standing on the Barrier Reef now," offered Mait, smiling. "You haven't seen anything yet!"

After settling in, they decided to kick things off with a sunset reef walk with resident biologist and naturalist Archie Harper, who offered daily tours to visitors. This would provide their first close-up look at the variety of fish inhabiting the reef.

Harper, an outgoing Aussie with a welcoming personality and big smile happily pointed out sea cucumbers, urchins, and crabs as they treaded carefully along the trail in knee-deep water, placing each foot so as not to damage corals, not to mention scraping their legs. After they'd listened and walked awhile, Rave asked Harper, "Have you noticed changes here?"

Harper's cheerful demeanor turned sour, a shadow flickered over his face. He launched into an impassioned, heavily accented monologue. "We're standing on top of the world's largest reef system; one of the most biodiverse ecosystems on Earth. The reef spreads across 134,000 square miles of the Coral Sea, made of over 2,500 individual reefs, and 900 islands. Yes. I have observed the impacts of ocean acidification here, and yes—warming sea temperatures are causing coral bleaching on our reef.

"The impact north of here is dire. The reef looks like a boneyard up there, and it's not coming back. Six bloody bleaching events since '98. Four in the past decade. You seem more dialed-in than many visitors, but I'll state it for the record anyway. These trends are unprecedented and scary. You probably know increased acidity harms creatures who live in carbonate shells."

"What does the acidity do?" Mait asked.

"They'll adjust to changing water chemistry within a narrow band," offered Harper. "But increased acidity slows clams, crabs, oysters, scallops, sea urchins, and amoebae's ability to combine calcium and carbonate and make their shells. They are slower to form, and the effort requires more energy. In extreme cases, acidity will dissolve those structures, and it's the same for coral. They become stressed and expel algae living in them when conditions become warm, or water chemistry changes. When they turn white, they're dead.

"When corals die, the reef does not come back. The ecosystem surrounding it goes with it. When it's gone, it's gone, mate. Too bloody right. The coastline begins to erode. A domino effect begins working its way up the food chain affecting fish, birds, and marine life. Feeding habits change. Biodiversity is lost, tourism shrinks, and local businesses close. And then . . . who knows?"

The group was quiet and contemplative as they continued navigating the reef walk. Rave thought back to the sculptures they'd spent time viewing back in Laguna, graceful dolphins, turtles, and whales preserved in plastic, stone, and photorealistic images. She felt a chill that caused her to shiver in the heat.

Tong began explaining their project to the biologist. "Harper, the reason we're here on Lady Elliot is to continue researching exactly the phenomena and change you just described. We want to find a way to raise public awareness and understanding of the scientific UNIPCC reports that are released every five years. They continue to grow in alarm and are backed by studies and data. But few outside academic and scientific circles seem to be aware of them."

Harper stared at the water a moment. "About bloody time. Glad somebody's doing something. Have at it, mate! I'll provide as much data as you'd like."

Once they were back on shore and seated at a table, Mait got her video rolling while Tong took notes. Harper let them video an interview in which he made several more key points. Staring into the camera he began.

"No amount of marine park protection can stop warming waters in the larger ocean. Think about it, mate. Occurrences of warming, bleaching, and change are not individual standalone events. They are connected by recurring changes driven by warming and threatening reefs in all oceans, the Arctic, Atlantic, Indian, Pacific, and Southern Oceans. There is only one ocean on Earth," he exclaimed, "despite different names humans call it in different areas."

Harper continued as the sun set, casting lengthening shadows from Lady Elliot's lighthouse far out into the Pacific until it disappeared as dusk settled over the eco-resort. The birds had quieted for the evening by the time the interview was done.

The next morning, the value engineers were up early, walking Sunrise Beach and doing yoga with Tong, waves gently lapping the shore. Then they headed into the café. Harper was on his second coffee, and the four of them got right back into it over servings of poached eggs and fruit.

Harper began: "How are you proposing to shape the data you've collected into a story people will watch?"

"Excellent question," Rave responded. "I've given it a lot of thought. A documentary film would make the most sense. We might call it: *Nature Won't Wait.* Despite all the environmental films already out there, it makes sense to put our research together into a script. I see that as the most direct way to capture what we've learned and share it with the public in a narrative conveying the growing crisis and its impact on every aspect of life.

"While we're here together, let's write that script now. Having it in hand will create momentum for what we need to do next." Heads nodded all around.

What followed for the next two weeks was a disciplined daily routine. Yoga and a beach walk at sunrise, coffee, then gathering around the "writers' table" in a corner of the café where they put together everything they'd documented, working to find connecting themes and tie a story together. They wrote and rewrote, over and over, until that story emerged, detailing what was being lost and focusing on what humanity might begin doing differently to adapt and thrive in changing circumstances.

When they were done, they each headed back to home—Canada for Kate and Mallorca for Rave and Mait. Rave began pinging anyone and everyone she could think of who had a connection to the film industry, movie financing, and film production. She figured if the timing was right and the story resonated, they might connect with someone who shared their concerns. UN backing for the project might also buy her some street cred in the City of Angels.

RAY OF SUNSHINE

Kate Tong, back at work at NC3 headquarters, received several disturbing updates from Cande describing rapidly deteriorating conditions around her Cayo home in Belize. Months of drought had been followed by flooding and crop failures wreaking havoc on the area. Food shortages had begun, and hoarding and inflation were rampant. Supermarket shelves were bare. Those with means were fleeing to neighboring countries and higher ground.

Tong felt the need to step out of her lane and offer help to Teresita; things sounded bad. Tong reached out to Rave for advice. They discussed it and based on Tong's recommendation, Rave said she could offer Cande a position as a value engineer. She would be the first full-time employee at Maps Private Value. With that opportunity as motivation, Cande extracted herself from Belize. She made her way over the Atlantic and joined Rave in Mallorca several weeks later.

Rave and Mait welcomed Cande to the finca and helped her get settled. Cande took to her new life immediately. It turned out she was a better instinctive archer than Rave, having taught herself archery years ago with a handmade hunting bow she shaped from a stave of local mahogany.

Rave had secured funding and a film deal in LA, and pre-production was already in progress in London. In the meantime, Mait most wanted to see if Cande might be able to help her remotely enable wireless data logging on the self-driving vehicle that had almost caused her death. Mait provided Cande with the license number and location where she'd last seen the car a month ago.

Autonomous electric vehicles employ neoVI data loggers that store vehicle data on a built-in SD storage card. A wireless logger might be used to exploit the vehicle's Wi-Fi or its cellular data connection, employing an integrated automotive gateway leveraging a bit of custom code scripting. Certain state intelligence organizations could exploit this automotive testing component in the vehicles and occasionally use it to capture data.

In this case, Mait wanted to know if the vehicle had been programmed to target her and push her bike over the edge of the cliff. It had been a perfectly executed ambush, one that happened so fast Orleans hadn't been able to escape the intended kill zone, or "get off the X," as she had been trained. With a bit of tech support from Tong's NC3 cybercrime shop, Cande dug in and worked on determining who had issued the aggressive, near-fatal computer command.

Cande kept after the project through weeks of value engineering training. Mait also trained Cande in the traditional art of Japanese Zen flower arranging, and the correct pairing of wine with food. Rave focused on helping her with her academic subjects, including communication theory, corporate research, financial analysis, economics, AI prompt engineering, storytelling, elements of value, Excel, interviewing skills, business writing, use of the veSIMM training app, and sales methodologies.

Rave and Mait added a varied daily routine of hiking, stretching, yoga, martial arts, and meditation to the heavy schedule. Cande began each day early, spending her first five minutes with the Healthy Minds app, working on her attention-based presence, focus, and awareness.

Somewhat to Rave's astonishment, Cande soon developed a couple of nuggets to share concerning the mystery vehicle. It turned out the self-driving car had been registered to a pharmaceutical firm—the very same one that had hired MPV in the first place.

Things got stranger. This vehicle had been signed out by an AI for a routine delivery to a pharmacy, then had gone dark for a while thereafter. More digging determined the pharmacy was owned by a shell company, part of a complex arrangement of third-party cutouts designed to thwart all but the most determined oversight. The new value engineer kept digging and turned up receipts leading to an organization known as GMISA. This was the corporation that owned the pharmaceutical firm. According to news reports, its flamboyant leader Bellony LaMarque lived on the island of Grenada.

It took more time and effort digging into GMISA's activities and pronouncements before they began to understand they had stumbled into a hornet's nest. LaMarque had made herself into one of the main sources of climate misinformation as GMISA grew and had become a leader in money laundering, bioweapons production, and other shady business dealings.

The attack on Orleans had been an AI-driven, remotely executed homicide attempt after Orleans's text to Mait had been intercepted.

Who were they up against here?

EYE OF THE STORM

After nearly a year of cutting footage, dubbing sound effects, editing, and narration, the film *Nature Won't Wait* was in post-production. Time for Tong, Orleans, Teresita, and Maps to meet up outside London where they would have an opportunity to view the near-final cut and provide some feedback.

The four of them took a walking tour of the massive studio complex that included screening rooms, production studios, soundstages, backlots, and administrative offices. They observed a half-dozen feature films in various stages of production. The tour ended in a large studio dedicated to their film, which contained all the sets, stages, effects processing, digital storage, servers, and sound labs to speed production and remain on budget.

The value engineers sat in a screening room viewing the most recent director's cut. The story came across as they'd hoped; it was moving, insightful, and educational. With the narration, music, effects, and editing pulled together, the result was magic. There were several weeks of post-production work left to complete and polish the final cut. Then Rave could turn it over to the United Nations, and marketing and distribution would begin.

Giddy with excitement, they thanked the crew and left to get coffee. Outside they were met with dreary English afternoon weather; it was raining and foggy. Rave pulled her waxed cotton Barbour jacket tighter as they hustled across the parking lot through misting drizzle. It hadn't escaped her notice the persistent rain hadn't let up for days, which seemed unusual for early fall. There had been reports of flash floods nearby, and flooding had shut down rail service on the London Underground.

They walked toward Mait's rented Range Rover on the far side of the lot when Rave noticed Mait stop and look up to study a spot in the sky. She too looked up in time to notice a small flash.

"MISSILE LAUNCH. INCOMING! COVER!" Mait roared. They ran toward construction equipment at the edge of the lot, diving behind a bulldozer. Rave covered her ears and opened her mouth to minimize pressure from the blast wave that would follow. Rave peered over at Mait; she appeared almost relaxed, lying on her side, hands covering her ears, just another day at work.

An explosion rocked the parking lot, shaking the ground beneath them. Dust and debris filled the air along with sounds of metal shrapnel and debris pinging the far side of the bulldozer.

As the smoke and dust cleared, Rave peered out. The studio was gone. In its place was a smoking hole in the ground, a shattered pile of fire, twisted debris, and rubble, rain already dampening the flames. Rave, Mait, Kate, and Cande checked each other to ensure they were alright. Just battered and covered with dust, no injuries. They stood, dusting themselves off, and surveyed the scene.

They performed a quick search for members of the crew but found no one. Soon, first responders ushered them aside as firefighters took charge, working the site. Police inspectors took their names and statements. Though they were despondent and shaken, it seemed wise to follow the lead of the British; when it all is lost and the chips are down, don't get your knickers in a twist. Keep a stiff upper lip. And brew up a nice hot cuppa, a spot of tea.

They boarded the now dust-covered Range Rover, which had survived undamaged. Rave drove the team into central London and checked them into a new hotel, the stately Lanesborough.

Located close to Buckingham Palace, the elegant surroundings settled their nerves, a respite from the chaos they'd left behind. After cleaning up and changing, they entered the hushed, nearly empty dining room feeling somewhat subdued. They sat silently beneath the enormous glass rotunda.

A harpist was playing in one corner, working her way through "De Falla," a Spanish dance from the opera *La Vida Breve*. Soon the calm of the setting began to have the desired effect. They took in the performance, captivated by the measured, timeless elegance of the sound. A round of champagne cocktails arrived, along with a tray of elegant salmon sandwiches, deviled eggs, an assortment of cheeses, and scones accompanied with double-clotted Devonshire cream.

Mait was first to speak. "I'm sorry. I should have seen this coming," she began. Despite their protests, Mait shook her head. She had more to say. "What I mean is, we have experienced a steady escalation in asymmetric attacks over the past few months. Mallorca, Belize, Steamboat. This aggressiveness extended all the way out into the ocean to a dive boat in Palau, and now here in London.

"There's been a steady drumbeat of opposition aimed at stopping us. We have no idea why. Perhaps GMISA and LaMarque have something to do with all this; we don't know. What we saw today takes the goddamn cake. If it is LaMarque, she appears very determined, with intelligence, resources, and deadly intent is serious about stopping our effing project. It seems she doesn't care who gets in the way."

A steaming pot of rhubarb vanilla tea appeared. Mait held her tongue until the server filled their cups, poured another round of champagne, and retreated. Tong and Rave both began to speak, but Mait held up her hands. She was fired up.

"This is bullshit, Rave. We have been so busy working on the project we've missed the forest for the trees. You know I don't like being on the defensive—it's long past time we began thinking more clearly and start going after this fucker. We need a new plan that puts us on offense."

Tong spoke up. "I agree. We also need a new vision now. We'll have to come up with something that fulfills the contract and delivers to the UN what they need. The mission has not changed, though loss of the studio and the production would appear to be a huge setback."

Mait was still not done yet. "I have a personal score to settle here, Rave. I will take the lead on our investigation while you three work on a creative approach to building a deliverable, something new that uses the raw climate research and data we still have in MPV's secure cloud. Let's tell the climate story we want to tell and get our work out there for the public to see.

"If LaMarque is behind all this, she needs to be taught a lesson and brought to justice. Tong, it's time for some of that persnickety Canadian intel ops shit. Rave, pass me another cheddar scone and the jam there too, please. I'm starving, and these are just amazingly good."

Mait attacked her scone. Everyone sipped tea and champagne while the harpist moved on to "Passacaglia," a Baroque piece Handel wrote for harpsichord that was hauntingly beautiful played on the harp.

The final notes faded gracefully, accompanying their somewhat tipsy exit.

BARCELONA

A plan began to take shape. Rave knew the goal had been to document Earth's current state and communicate to the public a vision illuminating a desirable, sustainable future.

While a film would have been a great way to accomplish this, there were other options. "What if we built a multimedia installation, something on a scale never before seen?" Rave suggested out loud. "A place where visitors walk through a representation of Earth's current state, then immerse themselves in different futures driven by decisions we might make, or not make today, so they could experience the impact of each?"

Tong thought a moment. "Yes. I like that. What do you think of the name: *After All Our Tomorrows: An Immersive Multimedia Exhibit*?"

They began working up the concept, seeking to merge technology, theatrical presentation, science, information, and special effects. The first step would be securing a warehouse or museum-sized exhibition space. Then they'd create the audiovisual and multimedia infrastructure, publicize the attraction, and sell tickets to offset what promised to be a staggering cost.

Tong suggested they create a mockup that would communicate the vision for the UN IPCC, sharing with them the groundbreaking concept illuminating years of scientific findings, and communicating in an entirely new way with the public and political leaders. She performed some quick calculations and set goals for the production.

She estimated they would need 120,000 frames of video, along with a soundtrack. The multimedia components would require 900,000,000 pixels of animation and graphics, 500,000 square feet of interactive display space, tens of thousands of super high-resolution LEDs, and more than a thousand Holoplot X1 speakers. Custom control software would have to be written. This production would require technical skills and capabilities Maps Private Value did not have. So another task began looking for contractors, specialist firms, and technical effects experts.

The cost? Off the charts. Rave would have to speak to her client about that, but she was sufficiently enthused that she seeded initial funding out of MPV so they could get started immediately.

Rave fired up veSIMM. The app would help her speed creative development of a conceptual storyboard. She began using it to map out the progression of experiences visitors might encounter as they moved through this immersive exhibit, dictating scenes and sequences, letting the software help organize her thoughts. It prompted her for context and detail, then began mapping out a production storyboard summarizing what she had in mind, along with a list of specialist firms who might be able to help with planning, construction, digital effects, software development, and project management.

Rave imagined stepping inside the future, seeing the faces of her family and friends move through scenes where she was immersed in the sight, sound, and smell of a disaster: drowning cities, burning forests, and ruined villages. It would certainly provide compelling and impactful storytelling.

The visitor journey would start with entry to an exhibit where each visitor's face would be digitally mapped in 3D. Each would see themselves in a variety of present-day climate settings as they moved through the building. Each visitor was digitally in the story. The story was about them, their home, their family, and their friends, set just a few years in the future.

The immersive experience would be split into two pavilions. In Pavilion One, visitors would experience today's challenges: baking heat in a sweltering desert landscape littered with dead animals and ruined crops. They would smell raw sewage from a polluted river. They would choke and be blinded by thick smoke rising from a burning rainforest. They would walk across a flooded city street with water over their knees, the current trying to drag them down.

A mosaic of images would envelop visitors in a 360-degree experience. Ultra-high-definition digital projectors with edge blending and color matching would join films, animations, and images together delivering seamless views of every kind of wildland fire, flood, hurricane, punishing wind, and disaster.

Seventy-seven projectors would run in tandem, creating scenes thirty feet high and one hundred and eighty feet wide crossing the building's floors, walls, and columns. Visitors would be touring their world of 2034 where average global temperatures had risen two degrees because humanity failed to take appropriate action when they had the chance.

Visitors would navigate to the future of their own home, wherever it was in the world, and see how it had fared over time, or they could experience a glacier calving into the sea. Or stand a moment in the utter silence of a rainforest devoid of plants, birds, insects, or animals.

In the second pavilion, visitors moved from the "journey of despair" to a hopeful vision of the future where solutions had been implemented in time because of climate action citizens took in the late 2020s once they began working together and performing work catapulting them beyond the lassitude of their leaders. These survivors overcame disinformation that had once been aggressively promoted by so many of those invested in business as usual.

The team wanted to make the point that the solutions humanity needed were readily available, nothing new needed to be invented. This part of the experience would display how those efforts slowed the crisis. Growing food locally with regenerative agriculture. Insulating homes. Preserving forests, oceans, and rivers so they might heal on their own. The rapid adoption of other types of energy was key. Visitors would see themselves in the story. It was terrifyingly personal and compelling while at the same time encouraging energy and climate literacy.

When visitors walked out of *After All Our Tomorrows,* Rave's team wanted them to start driving changes in behavior and setting new expectations. Visitors would grasp the significance of the crisis. They would know there was hope and the time to begin making a change was now.

They kept the construction effort under wraps as long as possible. After a bit of brainstorming, they agreed Barcelona would be a good place to host the first installation. Hopefully, the exhibition would catch on and other locations might open in the future.

After scouting locations across Barcelona, from Antoni Gaudi's Park Guell to Olympic Harbor, they found the perfect spot. An abandoned beach club on the Barceloneta boardwalk, one that had sufficient space, power, amenities, and a location supporting foot traffic in a popular location. It was perfect.

As the pavilion came together with the technology and content, some of the contractors found it emotionally overwhelming being in there while building it. There was a fine line between rubbing people's faces in the current crisis to make a point versus promoting virtual disaster tourism.

Rave was amazed at the storytelling power of the multimedia installation. How compelling the three-dimensional visuals were, and how the story was driven by its soundtrack, animated projections, and interaction of lights with the imaginations of the visitors. It was as if scientific research had been deconstructed and cut back together the way a DJ might tell a story synchronized to a compelling beat.

When early visitors began watching themselves perishing in catastrophic disasters, their screams of terror and fear were real. When they stood helpless watching family and neighbors form lines at food kitchens and refugee camps shuffling in despair the burden of losing everything and everyone felt crushed with each labored step. Some could barely breathe. For many, it was too much. The production team and construction crews had begun to call it the "drag them through broken glass" pavilion, as it made visitors feel the pain of the current state in ways they had never imagined to be part of their lives.

Experiencing disaster up close was so overwhelming some visitors may not even make it to the second, more hopeful future pavilion.

Rave realized they'd need emergency medical services on standby for those overcome with emotion by what they were experiencing.

LOW-RISE GENES

After All Our Tomorrows sold out minutes after opening, accelerated by social media.

Once she got word, Bellony LaMarque requested her top lobbyist in Brussels, Max Tiburon, attend and reconnoiter the exhibit, seeking vulnerabilities she may wish to exploit so she could shut the thing down.

As a former U.S. Marine, it struck Tiburon as a too-easy assignment. He had seen his share of mayhem, bodies burned and broken in combat. He was no stranger to the catastrophic impact of modern war and disasters. He'd not given much thought to climate change though.

As a new dad, he had noticed his views on things beginning to change. Rather than thinking only of himself, a too-familiar habit, he'd begun considering what sort of future his two-year-old daughter might have and what the world she would one day inhabit might look like. He hadn't thought much about that before.

Tiburon moved through the first pavilion. He was immersed in various disasters including an experience watching his neighbors emerge from their homes and collapse in the street, victims of a deadly pandemic. Their immune systems, suffering from excessive smoke inhalation already, had been overwhelmed by a new flu strain that jumped from birds to humans. Most susceptible were those already weakened by ingesting bioaccumulated chemicals over many years of eating highly processed foods.

Tiburon stood transfixed, watching the scene play out, not quite believing what he was seeing. His worst nightmares doom-scrolled before his eyes, overlayed with layers of facts, trends, and data. It hit him hard. He watched as his world—the world he was leaving behind for his daughter—crumbled. Tiburon had been in advanced military simulators for training, but nothing prepared him for what he experienced here. He was sweating. It began to dawn on him what was at stake finally, and why some people were making a fuss about it. Additional scenarios took him on a walk through a burning Belize rainforest, a place he remembered from training briefly with British commandos at BATSUB. He was further shaken watching animals on fire bleating and screaming, panic-stricken, running past him to escape.

Tiburon found himself exhausted and dispirited by the end of his visit to Pavilion One. He was relieved to enter Pavilion Two and experience some positive future climate scenarios. The scene could not have been more different; it was like taking a walk on a pleasant day in the country. The sun was out, birds were singing, and all was well.

When he emerged from the end of the exhibit, the combat-hardened mercenary and thick-skinned lobbyist was sufficiently moved, and he'd forgotten about finding ways for LaMarque to destroy *After All Our Tomorrows*. Instead, he left the gift shop with an "I Work for the Whales" T-shirt and a colorful refrigerator magnet for his daughter.

When LaMarque read his report, she exploded in a screaming rant. Once she calmed down, she dictated a text message, firing Tiburon with a scathing text that insulted his work, explained he was highly overrated, blamed him for weakness, and then went on to threaten his family. The message ended by mentioning his young daughter was ugly and had no future.

Tiburon barely glanced at the text before deleting it. He was glad to close the door on that relationship.

In Skopje, Macedonia, another GMISA employee, Stojan Trajkovski, was trying to ignore his runny nose. There was no time to get sick; he was excited to take his young family on a too-rare vacation. The couple and their two young children were flying from Skopje to Barcelona to enjoy the city's beach, food, and sights for a long weekend. They were excited to visit the famous *After All Our Tomorrows* climate exhibit they'd heard about; his young daughter had insisted they see that first. His wife had gotten tickets weeks ago, and now it was time to make the trip.

Traj was a senior gene editing research associate at GMISA's biocontainment lab. He'd attended prestigious schools and enjoyed his demanding work. He was a good scientist, husband, and father, and didn't know the details of the business side of GMISA or the customers who purchased the lab's products. He was busy focusing on his demanding cellular biology research and building his reputation as a leader using CRISPR tools to push gene editing techniques further.

CRISPR, or "clustered regularly interspaced short palindromic repeats," was used to edit DNA sequences. The idea was to modify gene function and work to eliminate hereditary diseases. The tool had other applications as well.

Before heading out on vacation, Traj had one last task to complete. Whenever he worked on weaponized designer viruses, Trajkovski was careful to make sure he backed up the digital genetic blueprints to the GMISA private cloud. Cloud storage was managed offsite halfway around the world on the Caribbean Island of Grenada; details were handled by RX, the firm's artificial intelligence.

Trajkovski got his information uploaded. In the event of an uncontrolled incident in the lab, these backups would enable him to develop a vaccine for each strain he worked on. At least, that was the general idea. He'd never had to put it to the test. He hit send and headed out the door. Trajkovski wiped his runny nose and tossed a used tissue into a wastebasket on his way out.

After arriving in Barcelona, the Trajkovski family unpacked at Hotel Pulitzer. They took in the view of the city from the rooftop terrace where they enjoyed a quick lunch, then got busy exploring. They began with a walk down busy Ramblas, Barcelona's wide, tree-lined strolling boulevard where they ogled attractive shops, cafés, and kiosks. They made sure to stop at the colorful Mercat La Boqueria, the legendary farmers market. The kids' eyes widened at a mouthwatering array of seafood, meat, flowers, cheese, candy, and spices on display, gorging themselves on fresh juices and little cups of gelato.

Trajkovski noticed he was beginning to feel run down and unsteady. He chalked that up to their long travel day. He didn't give it another thought as he elbowed past thousands of visitors strolling tight aisles of the market. As he felt a sneeze come on, he buried his mouth in his elbow, to little effect. Aerosolized spittle flew sixty feet in all directions.

The family made their way to the harbor where they headed west to reach *After All Our Tomorrows* in time for their 3 PM tickets. Once inside, all were fascinated and absorbed in the imagery, sound, and visuals that embedded them in the disturbing current state of climate.

Trajkovski lost track of his wife and kids. He was drawn to a corner of the hall focused on an outbreak of zoonoses—zoonotic diseases that passed infection from animals to humans. Traj knew there were more than 200 known types of disease that passed from animals and humans. He'd carefully studied one of them, rabies, as a possible source of innovation in his work. The crossover from one species to another had been growing as habitat was destroyed and people lived closer to areas that had once been wild open spaces.

Traj was amazed at how real the effects throughout the hall appeared. The sights, sounds, and smells of accelerated climate change were compelling and disturbing. As he began to feel more ill himself, he thought perhaps it was from visual overstimulation. Or maybe something he'd eaten. Suddenly he felt very nauseous, like he might pass out.

Trajkovski violently doubled over, stricken with the most painful stomach cramps he'd ever experienced. He was seeing stars. He tried opening his mouth to call for help; no sound came.

A dribble of blood began running down his chin. His arms no longer worked; they hung limply at his sides. Inside his body, once-healthy organs had liquified to a smashed, bloody pulp in seconds. Trajkovski toppled lifeless to the floor, blood oozing out of his eyes, mouth, and nose. There was a lot of blood.

The hall was packed with visitors, and there was so much rich multimedia playing on the walls and floors it took several minutes before anyone noticed the prone figure in a corner, a rictus of horror etched onto his bloodied face. The body's dead limbs were still twitching involuntarily, beating out a macabre tattoo on the floor as random electrical discharges from brain-dead neurons continued firing spasmodically. Within Traj's dying brain, it was as if each neuron was a lifeboat marooned upon an icy sea, firing rescue flares into a dark, storm-tossed night. But these were lights no other human beings would ever see.

Then the screams began.

SMITE FLAT THE THICK ROTUNDITY O' THE WORLD!

Virus spillover raced across downtown Barcelona. The story dominated the news as the city went on lockdown, but it was too late to make any difference. Pandora's box had been opened.

Governments and health authorities have learned a great deal from the 2019 SARS-CoV-2 pandemic. Some would be able to implement community health protocols quickly. But this new and unknown virus strain would prove orders of magnitude more difficult to combat.

Cande, Mait, and Rave were at home in Sóller when they first heard the news. Rave sat down and fired up veSIMM. She began using it to try and peer ahead in time, modeling disease vectors, crunching data, and assessing climate impacts of a pandemic already more deadly and becoming more widespread than COVID.

Fearing the worst, Rave activated Banshee Mode in her app to simulate maximum impact. She correctly assumed spread of the disease would be rapid and lethal. Within the first week, her projections showed global deaths exceeding 100 million. At that rate, no one would have the ability to keep an accurate count. Institutions and societies would break down.

As her simulation unfolded, one-quarter of Earth's inhabitants—over two billion people—were projected to perish in three months.

As ghastly and depressing as that was, veSIMM didn't predict that as the end of the world. Quite the opposite. Sifting through data scrolling down her screen, it appeared this potentially large loss of human life might be the beginning of something entirely new for Earth.

As the simulation continued to play out, she noticed the AQI, the air quality index, become the lowest it had been in years. Fewer cars on the road meant a reduction in smog in cities from Delhi and Peshawar to Shanghai and Los Angeles. Fewer tourists, fewer flights, and fewer ships meant reduced emissions. Reduced energy consumption globally meant fewer emissions along with reduced demand for oil and coal. The air cleared rapidly.

A time-lapse video of the next century showed nature reclaiming half-abandoned cities and communities. Cycles of freezing and thawing eventually collapsed abandoned homes and buildings over mere decades. That was about all the time it took to wipe out many of the modern traces of human existence on Earth. Forests grew back and expanded, breaking up asphalt, concrete, roads, streets, and parking lots. Fox, deer, and raccoons were plentiful in what had once been thriving commercial downtown areas. Depleted fish stocks rebounded in the ocean, which was now several degrees cooler. Corals began to thrive. Sea levels stabilized.

The global reduction in economic activity improved every climate metric from air and water quality to global temperature averages, which dropped back to levels not seen since 1945. The Earth was healing itself. What did all this mean?

Rave kept her findings to herself. She was still trying to wrap her head around the implications when Mait interrupted her train of thought.

"You're not going to believe this. The initial outbreak didn't just happen in Barcelona, it happened inside *After All Our Tomorrows*. The virus moved so fast everyone inside perished."

They sat in stunned silence taking that in.

If there was any hope of pushing back this darkness, Rave was determined to find it. And in her gut, she knew that GMISA was the key.

The three of them sat down at the table and went through everything again. Cande began explaining new details they'd just finished putting together. "We used ChatGPT to parse social sentiment and news articles about GMISA over the past five years, Rave."

Rave nodded. "Go on."

"New patterns centered around GMISA, its work, and its public statements. We surfaced a snippet of computer code from the dark web that seemed to point to the self-driving car attack on Mait in Mallorca."

Mait interjected: "This all ties together. The attack pushed me over the cliff. The interference in our field research in Belize, Steamboat, and Palau, the attack on the London film studio. . . . It's all connecting back to this GMISA outfit. And the fish stinks from the head."

Cande continued: "That, combined with news reports of an alarming number of dead animals found last week outside a lab owned by GMISA in Skopje preceded the outbreak in Barcelona. The same virus was responsible for all the deaths. Part of its molecular fingerprint has been isolated at Tong's cyber lab. Here's the summary report."

Years of news reports concerning GMISA and its shady head Bellony LaMarque informed their findings. GMISA was involved with think tanks, politicians, and businesses; it had worked for years to block climate research, spread disinformation, and encourage one-sided research that bolstered its preferred narrative. It was invested in shady business ventures, including the manufacture and distribution of bioweapons. Mait and Cande had found the center of the spider's web; it was in Grenada. They had a target.

Puzzle pieces began dropping into place in Rave's mind. She sensed she'd need to confront LaMarque in person and find a way to shut down

GMISA's illegal ventures. What would be needed now went beyond value engineering. This was something else entirely. It was about justice and morality. It was about doing what was right.

Rave didn't say anything to the others just yet, she wanted to gather more intel and think this over. She strongly suspected the next steps would be hers to take alone, she couldn't ask Cande, Mait, or Tong to be involved in what was likely to become more direct, kinetic, and dangerous action, much more so than what Maps Private Value ordinarily did. The idea took Rave back to the military life she'd thought she'd left behind for good. These were now extraordinary times; they'd all just stepped into a new world. She had confidence in the conclusions veSIMM was arriving at. She believed in her judgment, skills, and ability to do something helpful, to find what the right thing was and do it. Something that would make a difference.

She imagined a leader like LaMarque would take care to backup data as sensitive as bioweapon DNA in a secure location. Based on her work with hundreds of eccentric, wealthy clients, she guessed those backups would be at LaMarque's headquarters in Grenada where she could easily lay her hands on them, rather than at a remote offsite location. With someone as twisted as LaMarque, ego and insecurity would trump disaster protocols and best practices. Every time.

What kind of security might LaMarque have? How rational was she? Rave would need as much intel as she could gather if she was going to infiltrate and neutralize GMISA HQ. If she was lucky, in one stroke she might find a way to stop the spread of the virus, bring a criminal mastermind to justice, and eliminate one of the world's biggest political obstacles to climate action progress. She chuckled to herself. Besides saving the world, it would also help fulfill her UN contract.

Not a bad day's work if she could do it.

Tong lent one more helping hand from afar, offering Cande a new lead she'd uncovered. A former U.S. Marine was living in Mallorca with a Palma address. Max Tiburon. He had a work visa on file that linked him as a contractor to GMISA.

Time to visit Max. Rave and Mait hopped aboard the Sóller to Palma train and were in town by early afternoon. The first thing they observed walking down Carrer de Colom, the main shopping street in Palma, was everyone was double masked on the street. They heard everything was going to shut down soon, so they wanted to move fast.

They found Tiburon's door and knocked, not sure what to expect. When the door opened it was easy to see they were dealing with a broken man. His eyes were downcast, he stood slumped and couldn't meet their gaze. He didn't seem surprised or even curious about who they were, or why they were there. Tiburon appeared to have slept in the clothes he wore, including a t-shirt that read "I Work for the Whales," and he did not smell good. He ushered them inside.

Rave and Mait's disciplined manner and authoritative bearing conveyed the impression they were visiting in an official capacity. They did nothing to dispel that idea. In his dark and shabby living room, Tiburon explained he'd been expecting someone might come someday to hear his story. He was ready to spill what he knew about LaMarque.

After two hours, Rave had what she needed: a background on LaMarque and her organization, a layout of the GMISA compound, and technical specs on the institution's knowledge management tools, protocols, and security. They thanked him and wished him well as they rushed to catch the last train back to Sóller before service was discontinued.

As it was, they were the only passengers on what was ordinarily a crowded train. They rode in silence. They had learned GMISA was a fortress-like villa. It included a large data center containing DNA blueprints for engineered viruses, along with a rogue AI named RX, malicious computer code, and a valuable library of climate research that had been withheld from the public for decades.

Rave needed to get onsite and have a look at all this for herself. There were several problems though. Already international airline service had shut down. Most national borders were closed. Such a trip seemed impossible at this point. Unless . . . she went by boat. Island to island, Mallorca to Grenada. Such a trip would involve singlehandedly sailing 4,000 miles of open ocean across the Atlantic, from the Mediterranean to the Caribbean. She estimated that with a capable sailboat and a steady breeze, such a trip could take three weeks or more. What could possibly go wrong?

Mallorca had emptied of tourists overnight; Sóller was quiet and isolated now. Rave and Mait took stock. They had a full larder in the kitchen and the garden had been productive all summer after Mait got it in shape, producing herbs, tomatoes, oranges, lettuce, and vegetables.

Rave sent Cande into town with a long shopping list including everything they could think of that might come in handy. Coffee was high on the list, along with dog food, bottled water, pasta, toilet paper, spices, oil, and a host of staples.

Things went along quietly and almost normally for a few days. Mait and Rave were enjoying coffee in the backyard on a lovely early morning. Despite the chaos they knew was out there in the world, you wouldn't know anything was wrong from the beautiful sunrise spreading before them. It would be nearly an hour before they began wondering where Cande was, and why she had not risen to join them on the terrace as was her normal habit. After a time, Rave went upstairs to check.

When she knocked at Cande's door, there was no answer.

Rave eased the door open slowly. She stopped and stared in open-mouthed horror at the desiccated figure wrapped in soaked sheets on the bed. Cande looked peaceful. There had been no warning, just a rapid decline leading to death. Like so many others.

Badly shaken, Rave retreated downstairs to the garden and sat heavily, sharing the news with Mait. Like almost everything, Mait took the news in stride, even as she had grown very fond of the remarkable Belizean who had lived so well, knew so much, and had been filled with such promise.

Rave and Mait stared at the ocean, lost in their thoughts.

Eventually, Mait drew a deep breath and tried to cheer Rave up, sharing a couple of funny stories about the work she and Cande had done together recently seeking the self-driving car.

Rave said nothing.

Mait then got up and went into the bar area beside the kitchen. She spent a few minutes filtering toasted sesame oil in a coffee filter, mixed it with savory fat-washed whiskey, added miso-infused honey and almond liquor, and then split the concoction between two cocktail glasses, each containing one very large square ice cube. She added a squirt of lemon to each to balance the sesame flavor with citrus. She carried the two cocktails out to the garden and handed one to Rave who accepted it gratefully while still in a deep malaise.

Mait asked her to stand up. That got her attention.

They faced one another and clinked glasses, looking each other right in the eye, draining the strong drinks in one go. They looked toward the sea. Mait began slowly intoning an old Scottish toast in honor of Cande and Rave joined in. They spoke the ancient toast in unison:

"Strike hands with me. The glass is brim. The dew is on the heather. And love is good, and life is long, and friends are best together."

Tears ran down their eyes, the two clinked their empty glasses once more, then tossed both over the cliff. Moments later they heard a faint tinkle of broken crystal far below.

They slowly trudged back upstairs, hearts heavy. Wearing gloves and masks, their eyes stained with tears, Rave and Mait worked together to roll Cande's body in her sheets, then carry her out to the garden. She hardly weighed anything. There were no words.

Rave texted Tong to let her know what happened. Mait called the Sóller authorities. It would be two days before anyone was even available to come. The village was at its limits for disposing of the dead due to the large number of virus deaths.

Rave slipped into a deep depression. Even though she recognized all the stages of grief, there was little she could do to shake it. She had been fond of the young value engineer. She stopped working and retreated, rarely emerging from her bedroom.

Mait had more experience moving forward with grief and loss. She knew to give Rave her space and so she carried on working in the garden, waiting patiently for her friend to rejoin the world. Such as it was.

Four days later, Mait was at the kitchen stove heating her hexagonal Bialetti Moka espresso maker. It was a calming daily ritual for her, ensuring the beverage was prepared correctly. When she finished, she would unscrew the small cast aluminum top and clean it with running water; no soap. All part of the ritual. She took her perfect cup of espresso and was heading outside when she noticed Rave, eyes puffy and red, navigating the kitchen in her pajamas and looking a bit lost.

Mait settled her distraught friend on the patio and went back inside to prepare another espresso. She heated a couple of day old Mallorcan pastries: a robiol and an ensaimada. The robiol was filled with cream and jam, and the ensaimada, a spiral covered with icing, was filled with sweet cheese. Mait rooted around in the back of the fridge and came out with a length of salty sobrassada sausage, which she cut and arranged on a plate with the pastries. She set everything down in front of Rave.

Rave stared at the food a moment. Then she realized how hungry she was and began wolfing it.

The two sat in silence looking out north over Port de Sóller and the sea. Once Rave finished, she wiped her mouth and said her first words in days. "It's my fault. I should never have sent her into town. I own it."

Mait looked at her. They were both familiar with loss and grief; they'd been here too many times before, grieving friends and colleagues. They knew you never got over the loss, but you could find ways to move forward with it.

"That's BS and you know it," Mait replied. "You couldn't have known, and you couldn't have done anything about it either. Get over yourself. Cande knew how to take care of herself, and everyone around her as well. She was damn good at it—we saw that every day here. You helped her just by bringing her out here. She was very happy right to the end, and you know that too. This was an accident; no different than thousands of other virus victims who've perished this month. From Cande's perspective, she couldn't have been happier these last few months."

Rave said nothing. She looked at Mait; she knew everything she said was true. Mait went on. "Okay. Here we are. What do you think the best thing is that you can do now?"

Rave sat silently, deep in thought. She and Mait both knew what the answer was. Rave forced herself to say it out loud: "Nail the bastards."

Mait smiled, and took a sip of her espresso, finishing the tiny cup in a single gulp.

"Welcome back, Rave Maps."

STORMCLOUD

Rave believed the GRBL Skopje lab had been a criminal enterprise from the beginning, funded by GMISA. LaMarque had her fingerprints all over it. What would be a way to slow the spread of this weaponized virus?

She weighed the options from a value perspective. On one hand, value would ordinarily be determined by weighing the pros and cons of a business decision. On the other, there was the arc of justice to consider. They were way outside the normal course of action appropriate to a typical business decision now. What went into determining right from wrong was a difficult equation to solve for. Though, it may actually be much easier, Rave thought, in the sense the right thing to do was often easiest to determine. It was doing it that was hard.

Rave swept everything off the dining room table with one big swoop; bowls, silverware, and mugs fell to the floor with a clatter. "Always wanted to do that," she yelled energetically to Mait in the next room.

Next, she pulled out maps and atlases from the library and scattered them across the table, researching the length of a possible singlehanded sailing trip from Mallorca to the Caribbean Island of Grenada. It was 3,816 nautical miles via the strait of Gibraltar from Sóller in Mallorca, all the way to St. George's on the island of Grenada. Hmm.

The next day, Mait and Rave took a long walk around the deserted port of Sóller. There were several seaworthy vessels tied up to the wharf. One caught Rave's eye—she had fine lines and appeared to have been well cared for, recently refitted. Rigging, hawsers, and sails in seamanlike order. Brass rails gleaming, her decks clean. Mait hopped aboard and performed a detailed inspection. With some fiddling and poking, she eventually declared she'd found everything "shipshape and Bristol fashion, aye." There was one more reason this ship appeared well-suited for the mission Rave had in mind. It was her name. *Stormcloud.*

At one point, Mait broached the subject of joining Rave on the dangerous three-week journey. Rave shut down that thought.

"No Mait. I appreciate it." She began. "I do. But I can't let you take this on, much as I would like to have you along. This goes way beyond anything we've done together at the firm in terms of risk and danger. I need you here; you need to look after the doggies and the gardens; it's what you wanted.

"I must do this alone, it's a personal grudge with me now, knowing what LaMarque set in motion. I want to stop it. I'll do it for Cande. And for you, Tong, and everyone else who has lost someone to the virus, or watched their neighborhood burn, flood, or sink. Can you support my decision?"

Mait was silent for a long time. She knew once Rave had made up her mind there would be no changing it. She'd said her piece; there was nothing left to say, and plenty of work to do. Without a word, she turned and continued piling supplies in the boat.

The following day the two of them ensured there was a full stock of provisions aboard, medical kits, flashlights, rope, bottles of water, fishing, communication, and survival gear. As a parting gift, Mait insisted Rave take a small box containing two of her prized Chris Reeve custom knives, which Rave accepted gratefully. Inside was a full-tang, dorsal-tapered Green Beret fashioned from Cerakoted MagnaCut steel, sporting canvas micarta handles Orleans had hand-rubbed with olive oil. There was a small sister blade, a folding Sebenza drop point. Both knives were built to tolerances precise as a Swiss bank vault. Mait gave Rave a serious look, at a loss for words.

"These knives will do good work in the right hands. I expect you'll bring me them back, Rave. See that you do."

SOLO

Life at sea sounded romantic and appealing, but Rave was quickly reminded of the reality. Living alone on a boat meant living in a state of omni-dimensional permacrisis. From rudder to rigging, the craft was often on the edge of chaos. Things seemed fine for one moment, but the next, she was scrambling to avert disaster. Weather, currents, wind (or lack of it). Lack of sleep. Navigation. Tides. Leaks. Fuel. Visibility. A lost shipping container could be lurking beneath the surface waiting to breach the hull.

The list of challenges was long, but it did serve to keep her mind occupied. If she was engaged in fixing a leak and improvising with materials at hand, she couldn't be stress-calculating how many people were dying out there or wondering about the health and safety of her friends at home and around the world.

Of course, there were good times, such as when the sun rose, the sea was calm, and her coffee was hot. She could look out to the horizon and realize this was the best place in the world to be. Like everything, it was a matter of attitude, being present and aware. Breathe in, breathe out.

Rave's luck held. The weather was mostly pleasant throughout the three-week crossing. Her GPS worked, and she had sufficient water and food. She'd just finished taking inventory and had a few days of food stock remaining when she spied the southeastern coast of Grenada right where it should be. Rave allowed herself a triumphant shout that came out more as a strangled, raspy sound for not having spoken in weeks: "Yes! Nailed it."

She sailed smartly between the two cliffs guarding the entrance to the bay of the La Sagesse boutique hotel in Corinth, St David's, dropped sail, and anchored *Stormcloud* smack in the center of the small, protected bay.

Rave glassed the shore and her surroundings with a pair of 8x30 Steiner Military Marine binoculars. Seeing no one around, she locked the cabin cover shut, threw her backpack in the dinghy, stepped in, untied, shoved off, and rowed to shore. Rave could see the hotel had been deserted for some time. A victim of the pandemic; no surprise there. She pulled the dinghy above the high tide line and left it. She rooted around, seeing if anything useful may be lying about the hotel grounds. She was swaying a bit on her sea legs. It'd take a few hours to get used to walking on land again. The gardens were neglected and overgrown with flowering shrubs, heliconias, lilies, and bromeliads. She was able to scrape together an armful of yams, cassava, breadfruit, and several plantains, along with a few nutmegs wrapped in their lacey covering of red mace. She left the food in the boat.

Rave reviewed her rough plan. Her goal was to find a working vehicle and make her way thirty minutes along the Eastern Main Road to L'anse Aux Epines, where GMISA's compound was located, at the end of the peninsula overlooking Mt. Hartman Bay.

Upon arrival, she'd have to improvise. She knew the layout of the compound from her interview with Max Tiburon. He'd explained the security team, surveillance, and data center on the lower level. Everyone had, once again, isolated at home when the virus began spreading. Chances were good LaMarque would be home when Rave arrived unannounced. She had an idea she wanted to interview LaMarque and try to understand her position on climate, her history of illegal activity, and the virus that had escaped from her labs. That should be enough to at least get her in the door.

If LaMarque wouldn't talk to her, Rave would go to the authorities with her story. Rave was curious though, why had LaMarque worked so hard for so long to quash climate research over the years? Eventually, people would realize they were in trouble, one way or another. Wouldn't they? Maybe that wouldn't happen until the water was lapping at their front doors. If ever. Had this maniacal effort all been for money or power? Or was it an illness, a sickness of the soul?

More important than whatever LaMarques' twisted motives were, Rave wanted backup copies of the virus mRNA blueprints that should be stored on a server in the data center, at least according to Tiburon. That was the best intel she had. If she could get the blueprints out to the authorities, all that would be required to save people was to replicate a vaccine. Scientists could isolate nonfunctional strands of the deadly virus's mRNA spike protein and then package them inside bubbles of fat called lipid nanoparticles. Once applied, the vaccine would deliver new instructions to the body, human cells would begin to create similar proteins that their immune system would recognize as foreign, which would stimulate the immune response. At least in theory, that's how it should all work.

But what if Tiburon was wrong and the backups weren't there? An awful lot was riding on this point. If veSIMM was accurate, two billion people could die over the next several months if vaccines were not developed. Rave had to try. If she found the digital copy of the virus design, she could transmit that data to Tong, who would do the right thing. If Rave failed and two billion people perished in the next several months, the pressure on planetary resources would be eased. That reprieve, as horrible as it was to contemplate, would give those who managed to survive one final chance to defeat the virus, while also working to further reduce emissions and find alternatives to fossil fuels. If there was anyone left to do that work.

Either way, Rave figured she'd go out with a clean conscience. Should she not survive, she would die having avenged Cande's death and would perish holding up the highest standards of her firm: *Valorem Non Dormit. Value Never Sleeps.*

Rave had left a sealed envelope with Mait in the event she didn't make it back. The instructions were simple. There was a link to a music playlist on Spotify for a memorial she'd titled "Daughter of the Storm" containing the soundtrack from *After All Our Tomorrows*. There were instructions for a simple stone marker to be placed on a hillside in Sóller overlooking the sea, with an inscription:

"Here Lies Rave Maps. They Said She'd Never Stop Seeking Value for Her Clients. Well, She Has."

DAUGHTER OF THE STORM

Walking up the long entry drive leading to LaMarque's GMISA compound, the first thing Rave noticed were enormous callaloo leaves lining each side. Originally brought to the island from West Africa, callaloo leaves were an ingredient in callaloo soup, a dark green, iron-rich dish popular on the island. That's what she saw, but what she could smell was different. The rich aroma of simmering oildown stew filled the air. Another traditional island dish, oildown consisted of plantain, breadfruit, chicken, fish, and coconut left to simmer for hours in a large steel pot, usually hung over a fire on the beach.

Rave passed through the open entry, noting discreet surveillance cameras and a body scanner built into the archway, which opened to an atrium parking area. An assortment of scooters, motorcycles, and vehicles were parked there, including a glossy black Mercedes Defender, a Lamborghini Urus SUV, and a quad-turbo 8.0-litre Bugatti Divo, all glistening in the hot sun. She paused a moment to pull a protective mask over her mouth and nose, then knocked on the enormous wooden front door.

Silence.

After several minutes the door opened slowly. There stood an older, local woman dressed in a housekeeper's uniform wearing a facemask. She looked at Rave blankly.

"I'm here to see LaMarque."

"Welcome, Dr. Maps. Madame is expecting you," she drawled in her heavy island patois.

The mask concealed Rave's surprise at being recognized. She stepped inside and looked around, admiring the open-air walls of what appeared to be a central living and dining area designed around an inspiring view of the ocean. Waves crashed far below against the cliffside. The space combined the lush thickness of the surrounding rainforest with the open view of the sea in a way that was welcoming and inspiring. It was the furthest thing she could imagine from a high-tech data center and headquarters of a global criminal organization. But that was the point.

Moments later, in swept Bellony LaMarque. A fog of clove cigarette smoke trailed her across the room. No mask for her. She exhaled dramatically. "So, who do we have here? Ah, the famous Dr. Rave Maps, value engineer to the stars! To what do I owe this honor?" LaMarque did not pause for an answer. "You're far from home, Dr. Maps—you must have gone to great lengths to get out here. We didn't have many visitors before, and these days, truly not at all. Very impressive. Imagine! And at a time when most people cannot travel."

"How did you know I'd be coming?"

"Oh, don't act so surprised, Rave. My surveillance drone picked you up twelve miles off the coast. That was quite a daring stunt sailing here from, Mallorca, was it?"

Rave knew LaMarque was trying to throw her. But she suspected that as good as her intel seemed to be, LaMarque had little idea what Rave did, or why she was there.

"Nice to finally meet you, Mme LaMarque. It's not often I'm able to spend time with a senior executive such as yourself, someone who has managed so successfully, and for such a long time, to evade governmental oversight, industry regulation, media scrutiny, and legal accountability."

"'Scrutiny. Accountability. Oversight.' Such strong language. You speak in terms dripping with morality, Rave. So judgmental. So boring." LaMarque sighed, then glanced at her watch, an elegant, diamond-studded, rose gold Cartier Tank Française.

"Come. What sort of host would I be if I didn't extend to you the hospitality we pride ourselves on here in the Windward Islands? Won't you join me for tea? We have much to discuss."

The shaded outdoor patio was surrounded by bougainvillea. Thick ornamental vines provided home to a vocal mix of kites, swallows, and parrots. A maid in uniform sporting the red, cat-eyed logo over the words "Crisis Drives Change" poured tea that was a pleasing light blue color.

"The tea is a local specialty made from blue butterfly pea flowers," LaMarque explained. Spread before the pair was an impressive array of sandwiches in addition to plates of grilled fish, curried goat rotis, and chickpea doubles with mango, alongside heaping bowls of saltfish, lambie, and macaroni pie. There was a crockpot full of the oildown soup she'd smelled on the way up to the villa. An icy jug of strong nutmeg rum punch had been prepared with fresh lime, pineapples, and oranges.

The overall impression of LaMarque's home and headquarters was an architectural and luxurious indoor-outdoor living space, something likely to be featured in the pages of *Architectural Digest*. Rave did notice a few details that hinted at the villa's darker nature.

Artfully concealed behind enormous leaves of a rare, endangered *Danaea kalevala*, stood a guard sporting combat fatigues made of disruptive, multi-terrain pattern camouflage, a design popular with British special forces. She was barely visible and very good at maintaining discipline at her post. The red specks of the GMISA logo on her uniform was all that gave away her concealed position.

Hanging over the oversized fireplace mantle dominating the center of the room was an unstrung traditional yew English longbow and a quiver full of hunting arrows. *Good to know*, Rave thought to herself.

After tea, LaMarque offered a tour of the grounds. The villa was larger than it appeared from the outside. LaMarque seemed anxious to share everything with Rave. Perhaps she had a hidden agenda. *Or she could just be a megalomaniacal, wealthy, lonely manipulator, channeling her deceit and lack of empathy into lording ill-gotten gains over anyone who'll pay her attention*, Rave thought.

Though her anger was building, Rave maintained her calm, noting every detail. They began the tour in the library. She'd been expecting a small room. When LaMarque struggled to open the heavy door and pressurized air began hissing out, Rave knew she'd underestimated the scope and scale of LaMarque's acquisitiveness.

The library had been patterned after J. P. Morgan's opulent rare book collection, now a museum, on 34th Street in Manhattan. In the Gilded Age style of the nineteenth century, both Morgan's and LaMarque's libraries featured opulent, inlaid walnut bookshelves, and elaborately decorated ceiling murals. Great master paintings adorned the walls. An enormous fireplace stood as the centerpiece around which were arranged plush, Renaissance-style furnishings. The book stacks were three stories high, filled with thousands of rare leatherbound volumes and manuscripts secured behind hand-built twisted wire screens.

On display in the center of the room was a large book on a pedestal. As she got closer, Rave realized she recognized this volume. A singular copy of the bible printed by Johannes Gutenberg in 1455. It was one of only three in existence. The momentous, surprising collection explained the dehumidified, pressurized air. Dehumidification would be critical to preserving these priceless works here. Just having them in this humid climate alone was a librarian's worst nightmare.

Besides that carelessness, all of this should be made available to the public. Rave was fuming now. No one was able to visit these treasures while they were locked away. Which was precisely LaMarque's motivation. Exclusivity. Hoarding. Possession for its own sake. Collector mania is taken to an absurd extreme. These were signs of an unbalanced mind, there was no doubt now.

Next, they peeked into an adjoining room.

"Oh, this might interest you, Rave," LaMarque said cruelly before pointing out the stacks of climate research that had been withheld from the public for the past forty-five years. Some of the material consisted of books, reports, and samples. More recent material was digital, stored in racks of humming computer servers. A label over one server indicated it belonged to the GBRL lab in Skopje.

Bingo, Rave thought, trying to tune out LaMarque's ramblings. That'd be the digital backup vaccine designs and protein subunits Rave had come all this way for. She did not interrupt LaMarque, who continued describing her collection, sounding more unhinged with each utterance. Her eyes blazed with a mixture of excitement and stimulation almost sexual in nature—she took such great pleasure knowing she'd kept everything locked up and hidden from everyone for so long. She continued prattling on, just as a series of waves headed toward shore could not stop once they'd gotten started.

"A shame the world can never know the truth. Every report points to rising emissions and a warming world. Some of the best academic, scientific, and investigative journalism dating back to the 1980s is here preserved for posterity. I own it all, it's mine. I can do as I please with it."

"Posterity?" Rave shot back. She couldn't help herself, she was angry seeing all the lost knowledge sitting here, useless and shut away from the leaders and evangelists who could have done something positive with it. "Why? Posterity for who? Billions are going to die over the next several months from a virus you helped create. There's so much accumulated heat and pollution baked into the atmosphere and ocean right now that temperatures will continue rising even if we could shut everything off now. Why did you do this? What were you thinking? I'd love to know."

"Rave," LaMarque said her name dismissively as if talking to a pet. "I'm sure I don't know what you mean. I've grown GMISA's membership and revenues 1,000 percent. Member stocks are soaring, the business outlook is very upbeat, and we've encouraged millions of people to get out of the way of progress. Perhaps you'll come around to see things from my perspective if you have time to think things over.

"Now, I've enjoyed our time here together. I hope you understand, with everything I've shared with you today, I'd like you to remain as my guest. It's not safe out there, and this is where our tour ends."

They descended stairs down another level to the guts of LaMarque's digital operation lived. Rave saw a typical ops center layout, a room of workstations ringed by large screens. There was a quiet hum of activity, the air smelling of ozone and disinfectant, half a dozen staff members sitting at monitors viewing data tracking spread of the virus, security of the compound, global climate trends, and business status of GMISA operations around the globe.

Two guards appeared, flanking Rave and forcing her away from the hum of the computers and toward a dark hallway. Moments later, one guard held a door open, motioning Rave inside a cell-like room containing a sink, toilet, and bed.

"You didn't answer my question, LaMarque," Rave yelled as the guards retreated.

No answer. The cell door swung closed behind her and an electronic maglock snapped shut. She could hear an echo of her shouted question reverb down the long hall. There seemed little to do now other than get some much-needed rest and prepare for whatever might come. Rave lay on the bed and was instantly asleep. She awoke six hours later and began taking stock of her situation.

Rave still had her gear. Her phone; no signal here in the cell. A length of SurvivorCord. A sturdy Hanks Leather floral belt. Her Breitling watch, Palladium boots, and Sebenza folder. She sat up and surveyed the room. Maglocks only remained locked when there was a steady supply of power. She had been meditating on that point while she was resting. Rave listened intently, there was no sound from outside the cell. It was 5 AM. She slipped off the SurvivorCord necklace and picked at one end, managing to withdraw a single strand, a length of utility wire. She bent one end into a small hook and secured that to a corner of the exposed lock mounted above the door.

The wire was long enough to reach the only outlet in the room, near the door. Rave removed her belt and wrapped it over and around the wire, creating a thick insulating layer she could hold. She paused to listen again.

Nothing. She pushed the other end of the wire into the socket, there was a quiet pop and sizzle. The door swung silently open.

Rave threaded her belt back onto her pants, ignoring the burned leather odor, and quietly padded upstairs to the living area. She paused at the fireplace hearth, reached up, and removed the longbow and quiver of arrows.

She spent a minute stringing the heavy yew stave. That required she step her left leg through the loose bowstring, place the bottom end of the bow outside her right foot and against the back of her left thigh, handle pressing against her butt. From this position, she could use her left palm against the top end of the bow and leverage it toward her, pressing back with her hip as she slid the bowstring up to the string groove where it seated with a snap.

She stepped out of the bow, listening carefully once more. Silence. So far so good. She knocked an arrow and headed back downstairs to the ops center. There was a night watchman on duty, clearly bored, expecting nothing. Rave hid in the shadows, willing him to continue making his rounds, which he did, disappearing around a corner. She stepped up to one of the computer consoles and tapped a key.

It was password protected.

She placed the bow on the floor, sat in the operator chair, and thought a moment. Many IT system administrators never change the default password for their systems, it's too much trouble to keep track of them all. In this remote location, run by a maniac and guarded by the best technology money could buy, Rave thought internal system security might not be so strict about following security best practices. She typed in "PASSWORD."

After a heart-stopping moment, the screen blinked, and the desktop appeared. It took Rave two minutes to navigate to the firewall's "outgoing rules" setting and open a port for outgoing traffic. One additional minute to locate the IP address of the server behind her containing the virus backup.

She emailed that IP information to Tong realizing it was just after 1 AM in Vancouver. Rave sent an "Urgent. Check email," text to Tong hoping she might be awake and would act quickly. Tong texted back a "thumbs up" emoji. A minute later, Rave's monitor warned a large data transfer had begun. Data was being transferred from the GBRL Grenada server to an NC3 agency server in Vancouver. Perfect.

Canadian intelligence would analyze the material and ensure it was shared with the World Health Organization (WHO), Center for Disease Control (CDC), and U.S. Army Chemical Biological Center (DEVCOM), from which it would be distributed to immunology labs where vaccines could be developed and distributed.

Rave's work here was done. She shut down the computer, picked up the bow, nocked an arrow, and stood up to make her way upstairs when she suddenly smelled clove cigarette smoke. It was too late to leave—LaMarque stood blocking the doorway.

"Someone's up early, I see." She took a deep drag. "Were you looking for coffee, Dr. Maps? The kitchen is upstairs." Rave noted the taser in LaMarque's other hand. "Do you take one lump or two?" LaMarque grinned, finger pressing the trigger.

Time slowed. Rave heard the hiss of compressed gas as twin darts leaped from the taser. Instinctively, Rave released her arrow from a half draw, twisting the bow. This caused her arrow to tumble, tangling the taser wires mid-flight, sending them crashing to the ground amid a shower of sparks.

LaMarque stood with a fierce grimace, her eyes wild. They widened further in amazement as Rave's second arrow shot the burning cigarette from her lips. The rage Rave had bottled up over Cande's death, the voyage, the pandemic, interference in her work, and years of GMISA lies, corruption, and disinformation all boiled to the surface. She was fired up now, and a third arrow took flight in an eyeblink, pinning LaMarque to the wall by her shirt.

Emotion flickered across LaMarque's face as she struggled to free herself, waves of hate and rage surging like a boiling storm. LaMarque stopped struggling; she could not work herself loose. She began to realize Rave held her fate in her hands. LaMarque felt a sudden shudder of fear, something she had not known since her childhood when her mother frequently screamed at her over the slightest infractions.

Rave lowered the bow to the floor slowly, then raised her hands trying to de-escalate the situation. She unclipped the Sebenza folding knife, flicking the blade open with one hand.

"What have you done?" LaMarque hissed, a note of panic filling her voice. Rave came close, holding her hands up, waiting outside LaMarque's reach. She smiled. At that moment Rave felt her heart open and her pent-up emotion settle as she took a deep breath. Rave felt at peace for the first time in months. She found herself thinking of an ancient yoga story: *"The demons are at the door every day. Invite them in for a cup of tea; have the discussion. Let their evil be a reminder to you to remain aware, to practice compassion."*

The two opponents stood facing one another. LaMarque's head dropped, authentic tears of shame welling up as the enormity of her misdeeds crashed upon her. Rave's presence as an authentic individual representing a lifetime of living with integrity, building positive relationships, and seeking joy and abundance while focused so clearly on establishing truth forced LaMarque to measure herself in comparison.

She didn't measure up.

LaMarque realized in a flash of insight she didn't like the person she'd allowed herself to become. She had a glimmer of understanding she'd been driven her entire lifetime by unexamined codependency and trauma that began in her childhood. The dysfunction within her drove years of self-sabotaging and isolating behavior. All for nothing. Here she was, at the reckoning. She wept hard, wracked by sobs as understanding of the harm she'd done dawned for the first time. Rave was the first person to call her on her shit in decades, no one had ever done that. LaMarque was now so physically and emotionally spent that the arrow pinning her shirt to the wall was the only thing holding her up.

Rave was busy texting the police. She put her phone back in her pocket and slowly approached LaMarque, who seemed subdued and resigned to her fate. Rave cut her clothes free. LaMarque slumped forward onto Rave, hugging her, still sobbing.

Rave allowed LaMarque to slide to the floor where she began rocking back and forth, heart filled with remorse. Rave stepped closer as distant police sirens could now be heard, wanting to offer the crumpled business leader one final piece of advice inspired by something she'd once heard Mait say.

"I'm here to honor your voice," said Rave. Rave paused a beat. "You have a lot of time ahead of you." Rave lowered her voice further, speaking in a whisper now, close to LaMarque's ear. "Plenty of time, lots and lots of time. Time to reflect and begin your long-neglected work healing and seeking inner peace. Who knows, perhaps we'll meet again one day. I'll look forward to seeing you in hell, Bellony LaMarque."

Rave backed away, turned, and left LaMarque lying there. She walked out to the entrance of the compound. A dozen Royal Grenada Police Force officers were rounding up the GMISA security team in the parking area. Everyone had masks on, and while it was impossible to read their expressions, the slumped postures of LaMarque's staff told Rave all she needed to know. They wouldn't be putting up a fight.

She pulled out her identification and headed toward the chief, the weariness of the long night settling on her. After offering a statement and seeing there was nothing more to be done, Rave walked down the long driveway, taking her time. Eventually, she made her way down the hill to St. George's scenic, historic harbor known as the Carenage. She entered a bar and café, one overlooking the water and the only place open at this early hour. She ordered a coconut rum punch smoothie with extra nutmeg on top. Sipping the icy drink, she sat and watched the sunrise.

A group of schoolchildren in matching English school uniforms walked along the edge of the harbor, laughing beneath their masks. It was the beginning of a new day. Just like the old days? Maybe better now, by just a little bit.

Rave was hopeful. She pulled out her phone and began drafting a secure text to Orleans and Tong.

TOP SECRET / HCS-P / SI-G / TK / FGI / RSEN / ORCON / NOFORN / FISA

RE: UNIPCC CONTRACT CONTROL NUMBER #S-2654 GLOBAL CLIMATE CHANGE: GRENADA / RESPONSE TO ONGOING CHALLENGES

Goal accomplished. Transmitted vaccine data. Subject in custody.

Impact of climate change visible in Grenada: warming seas, rising tides. Coral bleaching. Deforestation. Habitat destruction. Loss of species. Effects of pollution. Yet there is hope. I've seen it here.

Value of addressing Earth's challenges: Priceless. We helped make a positive step. One. There is more work to do.

The glass is brim. The dew is on the heather. And love is good, and life is long, and friends are best together.

She finished the rest of her smoothie. Checked her phone.

"Glad everything worked out over there," Mait texted. "Take care, come home when you are ready. Proud of you, Rave. Incredible job, unbelievable. You saved the world, my friend. No one knows. But I know. Plenty of fat-washed whiskey here awaiting your safe return. Doggies say hello. Keep me posted."

Tong also sent a note back: "Congratulations to the world's greatest value engineer! Rave Maps, you did it! NC3 sends sincere thanks. Canada's Prime Minister wishes to meet with you as soon as you feel ready. I'm so proud of you, as Cande would have been. You did well, Rave. Miss you, hope to talk soon. Let me know if you need anything. Take care."

Rave was in no hurry to get back to Mallorca. Maybe she'd hang out and work from Grenada for a while, at least until commercial flights opened back up. Hopefully, that would be soon.

She opened her Bullet Journal and began jotting down a few thoughts, trying to sum up everything that had happened, and what she was thinking now.

All our tomorrows will continue unfolding into the future. Humanity possesses the solutions it needs for climate action. Nature <u>won't</u> wait. It'll be working to reestablish balance where it can. If it can. No matter what we think or do.

The desire of many to enact change is on the rise. More countries are on board with sustainability, investing in energy alternatives, capping emissions, thinking long-term, and curtailing outdated, misguided policies.

The very real costs of doing nothing are dawning on business leaders. Environmental initiatives, carbon reduction goals, and diversity initiatives are part of executive and board metrics at many public companies now. There's a new focus on reducing energy consumption and minimizing carbon footprint.

Citizens are tired of waiting for action and are taking matters into their own hands, holding leaders to account, protesting, encouraging conservation, planting trees, protecting wildlands, and raising awareness.

There is momentum for change.

And still work to do.

SATORI

Two months later, Rave made it back to Sóller and rejoined Mait at the finca.

Health authorities had received the new vaccines and had been getting jabs into people's arms in record time across the world. It seemed the worst part of the virus was under control, though tens of thousands perished in those first few weeks.

It had been touch-and-go for a while.

Rave was up early the next morning. She sat alone in the backyard, warming her hands around a soup bowl–sized cup of coffee, listening to the birds, waiting for the sun to rise. She drained the cup and stood. It promised to be a gorgeous day.

Rave stepped over to her shooting position and hefted her bow, taking a moment to address the target. She squared her shoulders, inhaled, and drew. She held at full draw, centering her sight on the 100-yard bullseye. The sight zeroed on the center, then stilled on the very center of the center. She could release anytime. Still, she held. She was seeking something more.

The center of herself.

The center of breathing.

The center of the Universe.

She stood on the edge of opposing forces outside herself now, one pulling the bowstring, the other pushing the riser. Holding between earth and sky, darkness and light. Breathing in, breathing out. Being breathed.

She no longer needed to release this arrow. It would arrive at the target even before she released it. It had always been there waiting at the center for her.

She hadn't noticed until now the tears streaming down her face. She let them roll and exhaled. She was happy, and smiling, wracked by sobs yet experiencing pure joy.

She slowly released her draw, removed her arrow, and placed the bow back down on the ground. She turned to the garden. She would never pick that bow up again.

She didn't need to.

SOURCES

9News. "Costco evacuation due to Marshall Fire." YouTube Video, 1:16. December 30, 2021. youtu.be/wBJnBFDnaYE?si=d75cjvWITxrWnlQq.

BBC News. "Australia fires: A visual guide to the bushfire crisis." January 31, 2020. bbc.com/news/world-australia-50951043.

Brasch, Sam. "A year after the Marshall fire, Boulder communities are taking fire mitigation into the plains." CPR News. December 28, 2022. cpr.org/2022/12/28/marshall-fire-wildfire-mitigation.

Deb, Proloy, Hamid Moradkhani, Peyman Abbaszadeh, Anthony S. Kiem, Johanna Engström, David Keellings, and Ashish Sharma. "Causes of the Widespread 2019–2020 Australian Bushfire Season." *Advanced Earth and Space Sciences—Earth's Future: Volume 8, Issue 11.* November 2020. doi.org/10.1029/2020EF001671.

Encyclopedia Staff. "Routt County." *Colorado Encyclopedia.* December 4, 2022. coloradoencyclopedia.org/article/routt-county.

Hansen, Kathryn and Joshua Stevens. "Stress on the Great Barrier Reef." NASA Earth Observatory. February 27, 2017. earthobservatory.nasa.gov/images/89827/stress-on-the-great-barrier-reef.

Hosagrahar, Jyoti, Alba Zamarbide, Carlota Marijuán Rodríguez, Mirna Ashraf Ali, and Altynay Dyussekova. "Building climate change resilience and adaptation of the Belize Barrier Reef Reserve System (Belize)." UNESCO World Heritage Maritime Programme. 2022. whc.unesco.org/en/canopy/belize.

Intergovernmental Panel on Climate Change. "Sixth Assessment Report." March 20, 2023. ipcc.ch/assessment-report/ar6.

Lady Elliot Island Eco Resort. "Guest Sustainability Pledge." October 2019. ladyelliot.com.au/wp-content/uploads/2019/10/guest-sustainability-pledge.pdf.

McGrath, Matt, and Mark Poynting. "Climate change: Is the world warming faster than expected?" BBC News. November 17, 2023. bbc.com/news/science-environment-67360929

Pickrell, John. "Massive Australian blazes will 'reframe our understanding of bushfire.'" *Science.* November 20, 2019. science.org/content/article/massive-australian-blazes-will-reframe-our-understanding-bushfire.

Ramírez, Diana, Juan Luis Ordaz, Jorge Mora, Alicia Acosta, and Braulio Serna. "Belize Effects of Climate Change on Agriculture." Economic Commission for Latin America and the Caribbean (ECLAC). January 2013. repositorio.cepal.org/bitstream/handle/11362/26108/1/M20130001_en.pdf.

Robinson, Jancis. "Mallorca's wine revolution." September 3, 2022. jancisrobinson.com/articles/mallorcas-wine-revolution.

Travel Doctor Network. "Belize Air Pollution." February 23, 2021. traveldoctor.network/country/belize/risk/air-pollution.

Wikipedia. "Beetle kill in Colorado." October 2, 2023. en.wikipedia.org/wiki/Beetle_kill_in_Colorado.

World Bank Group. "Climate Change Knowledge Portal: Palau." 2021. climateknowledgeportal.worldbank.org/country/palau/vulnerability.

World Bank Group. "Migrants, Refugees, and Societies." April 2023. worldbank.org/en/publication/wdr2023.

World Bank Group. "Resilience and Conservation in a Changing Climate: The Case of Belize." March 24, 2021. worldbank.org/en/news/feature/2021/03/24/resilience-and-conservation-in-a-changing-climate-the-case-of-belize.

LEARN MORE

Books

Hawken, Paul, editor. *Drawdown: The Most Comprehensive Plan Ever Proposed to Reverse Global Warming*. New York: Penguin Books, 2017.

Klein, Naomi. *This Changes Everything: Capitalism vs. The Climate*. New York: Simon & Schuster, 2015.

Kolbert, Elizabeth. *The Sixth Extinction: An Unnatural History*. New York: Picador, 2015.

Thunberg, Greta. *The Climate Book: The Facts and the Solutions*. New York: Penguin Press, 2023.

Vaillant, John. *Fire Weather: A True Story from a Hotter World*. New York: Knopf, 2023.

Documentaries

Fothergill, Alastair Jonathan Hughes, and Keith Scholey, dirs. *David Attenborough: A Life on Our Planet*. Netflix, 2020.

Gameau, Damon, dir. *2040*. Climate Change Awareness Project, 2020.

Orlowski-Yang, Jeff, dir. *Chasing Coral*. Netflix, 2017.

Orner, Eva, dir. *Burning*. Amazon Prime Video, 2021.

Stevens, Fischer, dir. *Before the Flood*. National Geographic Channel, 2016.

Tabrizi, Ali, dir. *Seaspiracy*. Netflix, 2021.

Tickell, Joshua, and Rebecca Harrell Tickell, dirs. *Kiss the Ground*. Netflix, 2020.

Online Sources

BBC News Climate: bbc.com/news/topics/cmj34zmwm1zt

France24 Environment: france24.com/en/environment

New York Times Climate and Environment: nytimes.com/section/climate

Project Drawdown: drawdown.org

ACKNOWLEDGMENTS

Thank you, **Audra Figgins**, freelance editor and book coach in Boulder, Colorado. Your patience, vision, careful attention to detail, copyediting, and skill in thinking through the implications of story elements is remarkable. *Daughter of the Storm* is much better for your guidance. I learned a great deal from your work, and I thank you!

linkedin.com/in/audra-figgins-8157a5a0

Thank you, **Elina Vaysbeyn,** freelance book publishing marketing pro in Boulder, Colorado. You understood who Rave's audience is and encouraged me to use different approaches to reach them. You've taken Rave Maps' adventures to a new level for marketing and social media. Thank you, Elina! elinavaysbeyn.com

Thank you, narrator **Elizabeth Schmidt** in Los Angeles, the voice of Rave Maps in the audiobooks for *Daughter of the Cloud* and *Daughter of the Storm*. Your enthusiasm, talent, and professionalism brought a high level of excitement to the audiobook projects. Thank you, Elizabeth! elizabethschmidt.com

Thank you, **Robert Tucker.** Tucker & Latifi, LLP, Brand Advice and Protection Worldwide is a leading intellectual property law firm. Your encouragement last year was timely. I appreciate your years of friendship and support. tuckerlatifi.com

Thank you, **Mitch Globe.** Your interest in the story was critical in developing Rave's background, and your experience taking descriptive aspects of the book and re-envisioning them for the screen is exciting to watch unfold. Go, Mitch!

Thank you value engineer and firefighter **Isaiah Gomez** for sharing your experience and memories of life, struggle, brotherhood and camaraderie on the fireline.

Thank you, **Mike Whitacre** for your encouragement and great story suggestions, several of which appear in this volume, and more of which show up in *Daughter of Mars*.

Thank you, **Mike and Danielle Skov**, owners of my favorite Indy bookstore, **Off the Beaten Path in Steamboat Springs, Colorado** for your support and encouragement. steamboatbooks.com

Thank you to my many friends, readers and supporters in Steamboat Springs, Colorado.

Thank you to my innovative and dedicated value engineering colleagues all around the world at BMC Software.

What might the future have in store for Rave Maps, Mait Orleans, and Kate Tong?

In 2023, the world's first novel about value engineering *Daughter of the Cloud,* found Rave Maps, Mait Orleans and Kate Tong raising the profile of value engineering, drawing attention to women in technology, and learning about partnering and combatting advanced artificial intelligence. In the 2024 sequel *Daughter of the Storm,* the kickass trio, aided by Cande Teresita and others draw attention to the scientific work of the UN Intergovernmental Panel on Climate Change, share concerns about the risks of a changing climate along with unchecked emissions and zoonotic diseases. The characters take an opportunity to incorporate sustainable habits and decisions into their lives. So What might be left for the value engineers to do next? Plenty, it turns out.

We face a difficult challenge meeting the threat of fentanyl poisoning in the United States. Rave might get engaged next in helping the US government build a case for change—that fails. After researching the history of opium and the "old China Trade" tying Boston to Canton in the nineteenth century, Rave may be interested in paying both China and Mexico a visit. Maybe Rave and Mait are captured by a cartel kingpin. There's the unresolved issue of the chip housing AI Digital Maps still sitting on the surface of Mars marinating in ideas about the future. There's a chance Rave could be caught up in a surge in new Martian space tourism, joining on a dangerous trip that caters to wealthy adventurers seeking unregulated pleasures. Pleasures beyond the reach of earthly laws. A story covering these topics would have to have a title something like: ***Daughter of Mars: A Maps Private Value Thriller.***

Thank you for reading! I hope you enjoyed *Daughter of the Storm.*

Alden Globe
Steamboat Springs, Colorado.
January 2024

DAUGHTER OF MARS

A MAPS PRIVATE VALUE THRILLER

ALDEN GLOBE

ONE PILL KILL

One tap on the screen.

That was all it took to kill fourteen-year-old Tyler Sindal.

Tyler did not know he was dead yet. It would be two more days before the small brown envelope containing six blue M30 Oxy—fake pharmaceuticals pressed to look identical to prescription Oxycontin —that he had ordered on Whisper would arrive in his parents' mailbox.

The $5 pills had been mixed from synthetic drug analog powders in a filthy, makeshift criminal lab in Shanghai.

The automated pill press that created pills from that powder stood on a table in an under-construction retail storefront, next to a gas station in a whitewashed strip mall on the touristy Mexican island of Cozumel. Here those imported powders were combined with other synthesized poisons and pressed in a machine capable of processing several hundred thousand fake pills per hour.

Finished packs of pills were tightly wrapped in carbon paper, plastic, and tape to prepare them for shipment to the U.S. Carbon paper helped put drug-sniffing dogs off the scent.

Tyler did not know any of this. Didn't all pills look and work the same? He had seen adults take every manner of pill for a variety of ailments his entire life. It wasn't a big deal. At school, friends pointed out common emojis and helped decode them:

- The capital letter "P" meant Percocet or Perc
- The little school bus emoji meant "Xanax," (carts, sharks, yellow)
- A train on a track: Adderall, or Addys
- A bomb emoji: high potency

- A chocolate chip cookie emoji: "large batch available"
- Snowflake: cocaine
- Mushroom: shrooms
- *Chinatown, China white, Fetty,* or *blues*: Fentanyl
- Heroin was "roofing tar"
- "Crystal" meant meth

Tyler accessed the dark web via the TOR browser, swiping past weapons, girls, and children for sale, gambling, hate speech, get-rich schemes, and every variety of porn. He eventually found what he had been looking for: "blues." A couple clicks and his order was in. Six pills, $30. They would arrive in a plain brown envelope, looking like other packages his parents received daily containing household items.

Two days later he found the brown envelope in the mailbox when he came home from school. His parents were still at work and would not be home until late. He took the envelope upstairs and opened it in his bedroom.

It was almost 8:00 AM the next morning before his groggy, overworked parents began wondering why Tyler had not come down for breakfast. When his mom went upstairs to check he appeared to be asleep at his desk, slumped over his open laptop. A loop of Halle Bailey singing "For the First Time" was playing. The song was from *The Little Mermaid,* a film he'd watched babysitting his sister yesterday.

Tyler's mom dropped her mug and coffee splattered across the wood floor. Mouth open, eyes wide, she stared. Couldn't catch her breath. She struggled to process the impossible scene before her. She wanted to scream; she tried. No sound would come. Eventually, she managed a whimper that turned into a long, tortured wail. A horrible sound, like something that might come from a wounded animal.

Last week had been Tyler's fourteenth birthday.

It had also been his last.

ABOUT THE AUTHOR

 Alden Globe is a lifelong reader of thrillers, history, and biographies along with inspiring tales of adventure, travel, and discovery. He grew up in Marblehead, Massachusetts, obtained a bachelor's degree in philosophy from Victoria College at the University of Toronto, and studied law at the University of New Hampshire. He attended executive education at Harvard Business School. His career focuses on speeding access to critical knowledge that improves the performance of frontline staff including pilots, customer service, and IT professionals. Globe has been recognized for technical innovation by *IABC, Multimedia Magazine, MISQ, Computerworld, Smithsonian,* US West, J.D. Edwards, Microsoft, Jeppesen a Boeing Co., and BMC Software. He lives in Steamboat Springs, Colorado. Email: alden.globe@gmail.com.

Keep in touch:

- Website: aldenglobe.godaddysites.com
- Instagram: @aglobe
- Threads: @aglobe@threads.net
- LinkedIn: linkedin.com/in/aldenglobe
- Facebook: facebook.com/AldenGlobeAuthor
- Amazon: amazon.com/stores/author/B002BLQ4L0?ingress=0&visitId=fbbf4f9f-9d38

Listen to the Daughter of the Storm **playlist on Spotify. Music inspired by characters, locations and scenes in** *Daughter of the Storm*: shorturl.at/deTY5

Made in the USA
Coppell, TX
23 March 2024

30459487R00095